
⭐

"Blood? Did my head bleed that much?"

"Your head didn't bleed at all even though you've got a nasty lump. Someone stabbed you in the back."

"Stabbed me!?" Shades of Fulton Ridenhour! "What with?"

"It seems to be some kind of a knife. What saved you was it glanced off a rib and didn't hit any vital organ. But it bled like crazy. So your assailant probably thought he'd struck a fatal blow."

I couldn't believe this. It hadn't occurred to me that I was in any danger.

"Who do the police think did it?"

"Right now, Tommi, the theory is someone noticed the door was open, sneaked in to steal something, then saw you and hit you over the head. To make sure you couldn't identify them later, they stabbed you as well. Robberies are turning more lethal these days."

⭐

Previously published Worldwide Mystery title by
NANCY GOTTER GATES

WHEN PUSH COMES TO DEATH

DEATH AT PLAY

Nancy Gotter Gates

WORLDWIDE®

TORONTO • NEW YORK • LONDON
AMSTERDAM • PARIS • SYDNEY • HAMBURG
STOCKHOLM • ATHENS • TOKYO • MILAN
MADRID • WARSAW • BUDAPEST • AUCKLAND

For all the men and women who make history come alive by reenacting the Revolutionary War battles

Recycling programs
for this product may
not exist in your area.

DEATH AT PLAY

A Worldwide Mystery/January 2010

First published by Alabaster Books.

ISBN-13: 978-0-373-26698-2

Acknowledgments

For Stan Squires, Jeff Lambert, and Stuart Steele who gave me insight into the lives of reenactors, Lois and Dorie Crowe who helped me understand the world of showing dogs, for Tom Shulz for medical information, and David Spangler for his legal expertise.

And, as always, for the invaluable feedback from the members of my writers' group: Diane Berry, Elizabeth DiMeo, Helen Goodman, and Dorothy P. O'Neill.

ONE

I WAS LATE FOR the condo association board meeting, feeling a little embarrassed because it was my first one, and I wasn't making a very good impression. But Tee, short for Tee-nine-cy, my corpulent brown Maine Coon cat, had barfed on my pale beige carpet just before I was supposed to leave. I knew if I didn't clean it up right then I'd have a big brown stain in the middle of the living room. He'd been a stray before I adopted him, and he gobbles up his food like there is no tomorrow, fearful he might miss his next meal. Unfortunately he usually eats more than his stomach can hold. Bless his big furry heart.

The president of the board eyed me with disapproval as I tried to slip unnoticed into the one vacant seat around the table. I knew that her name was Rhonda Worthington although I had never met her; but her reputation as a formidable figure had spread far and wide throughout the neighborhood. She ruled the association as though she were the CEO of a Fortune 500 company, with insufferable hauteur.

The meeting had already begun. She was discussing pool maintenance and stopped in mid-sentence when the legs of my chair screeched loudly as I pulled it out from the table. "I believe you are Tommi Poag?" she asked, her unctuous voice not quite disguising her impatience.

"That's me," I said, feeling my face turn pink. "I had a minor catastrophe at home." I wasn't going to embarrass myself by telling them my cat threw up.

She gave me a rather stony look as if I'd interrupted the State of the Union address. "That's too bad," she said sounding not in the least sorry. "Now, let's get on with our business."

I had agreed to join the board with a great deal of reluctance. My next-door neighbor on Cottage Place had served on it for years and felt the only way she could bow out gracefully was to recruit someone to take her place. I think I was about the tenth person she asked, and she caught me at a time my resistance was low. It was February, and every year about this time I become utterly fed up with cold weather, gray skies, and bleak landscapes. My good humor index hits a low, and I was looking for something to distract me from my grumpiness. Why I thought joining a board that is bound to be contentious was the thing to do I'll never know.

I soon found out what I was in for. The board members argued about the lawn maintenance, the proposed assessment for repairing cracked sidewalks, the ban against painting the front door any color other than white, and other even less compelling matters. Most items of business were continued until the next board meeting without resolution. I wondered if they thought if they postponed them enough times, they might just go away.

I kept a low profile throughout the meeting, feeling that I needed time to study the issues before I opened my mouth. Others seemed to have no qualms about speaking up, even when it was evident they didn't know what they were talking about. I was beginning to regret my decision already.

Finally the meeting was over, and the members were invited to stay and have coffee and brownies. I hung around in hopes they might seem more likable on a social level than they did while discussing the business of the homeowners' association.

There are over seventy-five townhouses in our association, and I knew only one or two members of the board and then only to say hello if I passed them on the street. Since I work in a life insurance office, I don't have the time or inclination to become very involved with condo social activities which are usually attended by families with children and/or couples. As a divorcee, I felt like the odd-woman-out most of the time. The only single men I knew there were Colin and Sean, a gay couple who were probably the friendliest neighbors around. I always attended their Christmas party that was the highlight of the season.

I grabbed a cup of coffee and a brownie and began to circulate. I approached a woman who was the only one who appeared to be older than I, that is to say over fifty-nine. She had pure white hair cut like a man's, but I didn't think she was much past her early sixties. She had the slender build of a teenager, and while her skin was glowing and smooth, she didn't have the taut look that would suggest she'd had cosmetic surgery. I surmised she took excellent care of herself, something I don't seem to have the time or inclination to do. I'm a little on the slothful side when it comes to beauty routines. Hanging on a cord around her neck were the granny glasses that she had used during the meeting when reading a request from a resident who wanted to paint her door barn red.

Rhonda had turned down the request without discussion. "It's in our bylaws that all doors have to be white," the president had insisted as if they were written in stone. "We'd have to get a majority vote from the whole association to change it, and I can't see that it would be worth our time to go to that much trouble for one person."

I could tell the woman was furious at the response, but she managed to accept defeat with grace. Maybe she was planning to rally support for the next meeting.

I introduced myself and asked her name.

"Constance Merritt," she said. "So good to see a new face on the board. We could sure use some fresh ideas."

"I don't know about fresh," I said. "Sometimes I think my brain is curdling from disuse. I have a job where the main thing I need to know is the alphabet so I can file, and I think I learned that in kinder-garten."

That wasn't completely true, but I guess it's human nature to badmouth one's job. I like my job well enough, and I'm very fond of my boss. And I do more than filing. Logan had hired me because I knew how to use a computer which his seventy-five-year-old recently retired secretary did not. My job not only gives me necessary income, but it kept me occupied while I went through a bitter divorce over two years earlier. Otherwise I would have been sitting at home dwelling on ways to get even with Bernard, my wayward ex-husband. But I've finally emanci-pated myself from my anger at him, and I'm perfectly happy to let his wife, Pamela, suffer his ego and his peculiar ways.

Constance and I chatted for a while about the topics that were discussed at the board meeting, and we seemed to see eye-to-eye on them, which was the opposite of the stand that the president and the majority of board members took.

"Will we just be butting our heads against the wall?" I asked her. "I hate to waste my time if I'm going to be voted down on everything."

"You know, we need to talk about that, develop a strategy," she said. "I've got to run tonight, but maybe we can get together sometime and discuss it."

"Sure," I said. "Give me a call." And I gave her my phone number.

AND THAT WAS HOW Constance I and became friends. We got together at her place soon after the meeting and discussed ways we might appeal to other board members to see another side of some issues. We knew we would be fighting the odds—it's so much easier to go along with the status quo than it is to seek change—but being optimistic souls, we thought it was worth a try.

Getting to know Constance made having to deal with the cantankerous board members worthwhile. She'd been a nurse for many years and had the nurturing personality one hopes for in a medical professional. Since retiring a few years earlier, she's kept busy doing volunteer work for a number of organizations including Mobile Meals, Urban Ministry, and United Way. She is one of those souls who gives of time and energy so selflessly, it always makes me feel somehow lacking.

I confided to her about my failed marriage, how Bernard had left me for a young associate in his law firm after thirty-three years of marriage. That had been three years earlier, and I'd finally recovered from the shock and hurt he had inflicted on me. Well, almost recovered. Once in a long while, I had a little pity party for myself. But those were further and further apart.

We were having a glass of wine together celebrating our collaboration when her husband came in. She'd told me he was off at a meeting of his own.

"Tommi, this is Garland. Garland, Tommi lives the next street over. She's new to the homeowners' board."

I stood to shake his hand. He was a fine looking

man with hair as white as his wife's. I guessed they were about the same age, and he had a rather majestic aquiline nose and piercing blue eyes. He'd cultivated a nice tan that made his hair look even whiter and his eyes bluer. They made quite a stunning couple.

"So they suckered you in," he said with a laugh. "At least it's good to know Connie has an ally now. I assume you are or you probably wouldn't be here. Most of the board members treat her like she's from the evil empire. They think she's always stirring things up."

"Well, they're right," she agreed. "I do. I get irritated with their laziness. 'Let's always do the same old, same old.' That seems to be their motto."

"At least our group can work out our frustrations; we just shoot each other," Garland said with a twinkle in his eye.

Constance said nothing, but could hardly contain her grin. I looked from one to the other. "You play paintball?" I asked.

"I guess you could say a version of it," he said. "Only in costume. And with muskets."

Constance winked at me. "Garland prefers dress uniforms to camouflage. He's a captain in the Continentals."

Finally the light dawned. "You're a reenactor?" I asked.

"Have been for the past twenty years," he said. "We reenact the Battle of Guilford Courthouse every March as well as a number of other battles on the east coast throughout the year. That's what our meeting was tonight. Getting ready for it."

"How cool," I said.

I had attended the reenactment a couple of times and was fascinated by the people who participated. They spent the weekend camping out before the battle, living the way soldiers and civilians would have lived in the late 1700s, cooking their meals over open fires, dressed as veteran Continental soldiers, Virginia riflemen, or untrained North Carolina militia along with camp followers. "General Nathanael Greene's soldiers" occupied one site, while "Lord Cornwallis's British troops" camped at another. I marveled at the dedication of these men and women to make every facet of the reenactment as realistic as possible.

The Battle of Guilford Courthouse, one of the most important battles of the Revolutionary War, is commemorated by the smallest national military park in the nation, a little over two hundred acres located in the midst of built-up neighborhoods on the north side of Greensboro, North Carolina where I live. Fought on March 15, 1781, it was a turning point in the war when General Greene's troops, although ostensibly defeated, did so much damage to Cornwallis's army that his reserves were decimated. The British then marched to the coast at Wilmington, giving up on their Southern strategy, and eventually became entrenched at Yorktown, Virginia where they surrendered to a superior force of French and American troops on October 19, 1781.

I turned to Constance. "Are you involved in this too? I see women and children at the campsites."

"No, I leave it to Garland," she said. "I always did like my creature comforts. Besides that, it costs a pretty penny to have authentic uniforms and weaponry. Some of the wives make them for their husbands as well as dresses for themselves, but I never learned how to sew. Garland actually took up sewing so he could put his own outfits together. Even then it cost more than an arm and a leg."

"Yeah, I've had friends give me a hard time when they hear I've been sewing," Garland said. "But I remind them that it's not that much different than their woodworking hobby. You cut out a pattern and put it together whether it's cloth or boards."

I tried to envision him in white breeches, blue and red coat, and tricorn hat and decided he would cut quite a dashing figure as a Revolutionary soldier. How much more interesting and colorful than the ubiquitous sweats or jeans men wear today.

"What made you decide to become a reenactor?" I asked. It seemed to me to require a huge amount of dedication and time to say nothing of money.

"I teach high school history, and the Revolutionary War period has always been one of my favorite subjects. Joining this group has made it come alive not only for me but for my students. I've always said if you talked to the men in my regiment you could write a ten-thousand page book about the details of daily life as well as the battles. We've all researched that time period so thoroughly that everything we do is as authentic as possible."

"Where do you get your equipment?" I asked.

"There are suppliers for just about everything. Have you visited the campsite we set up the weekend of the battle? Some of the tents house vendors who were called sutlers at that time. They carry all sorts of period paraphernalia, but a lot of us make our own muskets."

"How about cannons? Do you have your friendly neighborhood cannon shop?"

"Actually some of the men make them although it's quite a process. You can get drawings from the US Army Ordnance Division. And they often stow them in their garages, preempting their cars. I know one guy who keeps his in his driveway much to the consternation of his neighbors."

"That must be quite a conversation piece."

"You could say that."

"Well, it'll be even more interesting to attend the reenactment this year now that I know someone who's involved."

"Come to our campsite on that Sunday before the battle and I'll show you around."

"I'll take you up on that."

TWO

CONSTANCE CALLED ME a week later as I was eating my usual microwave frozen dinner in front of the TV while I watched the evening news. A cook I am not. I tried with limited success when I was married, but my heart wasn't in it. As soon as I became single, I decided that was the end of meals made from scratch. There aren't many ways I can afford to indulge myself, but since I don't grow my own vegetables or raise chickens to cut costs, I can eat frozen meals for about the same amount as if I spent hours in the kitchen. A good thing I don't have discriminating taste buds.

"We're having an emergency meeting of the board tonight," she said. "Are you free?"

"What's it about?" I asked.

"Don't have time to fill you in. I'm in the midst of getting dinner. But you'll find out when you get there. It's at 7:30."

I wondered what could be so urgent. My impression was that the board members would procrastinate over making decisions about anything, so what could have happened that made them have an unscheduled meeting?

Everyone was assembled in the clubhouse by 7:40.

The president had a look of concern on her face that replaced the annoyed but bored expression she'd maintained throughout the last meeting.

Constance came bustling in just before Rhonda rapped her gavel for attention.

"We have a crisis on her hands," she said. She pronounced it with such solemnity that I couldn't imagine what disaster could have befallen us. Had they decided to build a five-lane road through our development? In Greensboro, you never could be certain whether or not they might condemn your property for a new highway or build a strip mall next door. Residential zoning could be changed to commercial even over the outraged protests of nearby homeowners. Developers rule the world.

"We're being sued for a hundred thousand dollars," she said. "I already talked to our insurance company, and they say they won't cover it."

There was a collective gasp around the table as we took that in. I, for one, couldn't even contemplate the fallout that would result.

"What on earth are we being sued for?" Constance was the first to speak up.

"It's complicated," Rhonda said. "You know that we are having all the trim painted on the homes." Indeed we did. That was why Constance's friend had wanted to have her door painted red. They could have easily done it while they were painting the rest of the condo's trim. The siding varied from home to home: brick, shingles, even some fake stone, so the trim was the only thing that needed to be painted on occasion. This was good because it kept down the maintenance cost.

"Last week," she continued, "they were working on Fulton Ridenhour's place. Fulton was gone for the day, but we'd notified everyone about the painters and advised that they would have a master key to the front door so that it could be opened long enough to paint the edge of the door."

"Good Lord," I exclaimed. "Isn't that asking for trouble, giving these people access to all the homes?"

"We were very careful about that," Rhonda said as if I should know better. "We used our permanent maintenance staff who've been thoroughly vetted with background checks and all. They are all bonded and insured, and we know they are people who can be trusted. They've worked for us for many years."

"So? What's the problem?" Joe Kernodle spoke up. I'd heard via the grapevine that Joe was one of the board members who took issue with every suggestion that was made for improvements or changes to the usual way of doing things.

I'd wondered why he was on the board at all. If he thought it gave him any prestige, he should think again. My impression was that the majority of residents thought of the board members as a bunch of suckers who got duped into participating.

Rhonda proceeded to explain what had happened. "Fulton was out for the day when the painters got to his house. They were working on his front door, and when they opened it to finish the job, Sir Martingale got out accidentally."

"Sir Martingale? Who the Sam Hill is that? Was some English lord staying with him?" Joe was being facetious and wouldn't let Rhonda finish without interruption. I'd noticed at the first meeting I'd attended that he craved attention. Loved the sound of his own voice.

Rhonda was pissed now. She'd been agitated to begin with, and she wasn't about to put up with the likes of Joe. "If you'd just shut up long enough to let me finish, I'll explain it all."

Joe didn't say a word but looked at her with smoldering hostility, and when she took a sip from her water bottle I could see his lips silently forming the word "bitch."

Rhonda set the bottle down with a bang that made us all jump.

"Now listen up. Here's the story. Sir Martingale is a show dog, a very valuable one, an English Spaniel that won ribbons in many shows, including Best of Show. He was soon to be retired to lead the life of a stud and that can be extremely lucrative. In fact these dogs don't make much being taken around the country to participate in shows. The money is in the stud fees and in his progeny."

She paused, but no one dared to say anything.

"Someone in his block was changing his antifreeze. He'd drained out the old into a pan and was preparing to put in the new when his wife called him into the house to take a phone call."

I looked at Constance and she looked at me. We both knew what was coming next.

"Sir Martingale drank that antifreeze and it killed him."

Everyone was too stunned to say anything. I love dogs second only to cats, and I could imagine how devastating that would be, even if it had come from the pound. I know some people get more upset when a dog is abused or killed than they do when reading about the daily murder and mayhem that happens all around us. Maybe it's because dogs and cats love us so unconditionally and do nothing to deserve such treatment.

Finally Mack Thurston spoke up, saying what was on everyone's mind. "So Ridenhour is suing the homeowner's association for letting the dog out."

"You got it," Rhonda said.

"Why not sue the guy who left the antifreeze sitting there?"

"Because he had no expectations that a dog would come along and drink it. It's not against the law to change your antifreeze nor to leave it out. Dogs are supposed to be on a leash when they're outside."

"But a hundred thou!" Joe stormed. "That's ridiculous for a dog."

"That includes 'pain and suffering' and all that kind of thing," Rhonda said. "It seems kind of ridiculous to me, but our lawyer says it's no laughing matter."

"I get it," Mack said, "Ridenhour can laugh all the way to the bank."

"So what are we going to do?" asked Constance.

"I think the first thing to do is to form a small committee to get together with Fulton and try to work out some kind of a reasonable solution. How about you being on that committee Constance? You always speak up at board meetings."

I sensed that she did not mean that in a positive way, and I'm sure Constance did too. But the suggestion must have appealed to Constances's need for positive action on board issues.

"Sure. I'll do that," she replied.

"And you, Tommi. I understand you are in insurance. How about being on the committee as well?"

"I work in life insurance," I protested. "I don't know anything about this sort of thing."

"Well, I'm sure your experience will be helpful anyway," Rhonda said in a deprecating tone.

"Okay," I said meekly. If I was going to be on the board, I didn't want to sit around twiddling my thumbs.

"And Joe," Rhonda went on. "You seem especially upset about this. How about you being the other committee member."

"Yeah. I don't know this guy, but I'd sure like to meet him and tell him what I think of him."

I was horrified. Joe was going to doom the discussion before it even started with that attitude.

"Now Joe," Rhonda said, "You're going to have to

use tact and gentle persuasion if you hope for any success."

"Gentle persuasion my ass," Joe replied.

"Well, perhaps I should ask someone else…"

"No. I'll behave. I'll have these two ladies to keep me under control."

"Okay then. I suggest you get together with Fulton as soon as possible."

I was absolutely dismayed at having to work with Joe. He seemed like an idiot to me. I wondered if Rhonda had a hidden agenda and put him on the committee to ensure we would fail. But why on earth would she do that?

THREE

WE WERE ABLE TO set up a meeting with Fulton for the following Saturday morning. He worked evenings at one of the Home Depot stores so he wasn't available during the week.

Constance and I got together the night before to talk about how to best approach him. She'd invited Joe to join us, but he said he didn't need to "rehearse" his speech. He knew what he would say already. That really made us nervous. He was a loose cannon.

Garland was at home and we invited him to share his thoughts with us.

"I know Fulton," he said. That was good because neither Constance nor I had met him. Perhaps he could give us some insight into the man.

"And?" Constance asked.

"He's not going to be easy to deal with. He graduated from some little Podunk law school, but he could never pass the bar here. He's pretty bitter about that. Mostly because he's sure he knows his stuff. He has all kinds of excuses as to why he flunked it."

"Oh, Lord." Constance shook her head in concern. "How do you know him, Garland?"

"He's one of the sutlers at the reenactment. He

sells wool and linen and muslin to make uniforms. You can't go to a fabric shop and buy one hundred percent wool. All of it has a small percentage of synthetic in it which of course they didn't have in the eighteenth century. It has to be ordered from Holland, and you have to buy a whole bolt. Most people can't afford nor want twenty-three yards of wool."

I couldn't believe the lengths the reenactors go to to preserve authenticity.

"But how does he have time to do that and show dogs too?" Constance asked. "Both usually take place on weekends."

"He owns the dog, but he has a handler who takes it to shows. Fulton inherited the dog as a pup when his mother died. I don't think he's particularly into the dog show thing, but he knew that he could probably make a bundle off Sir Martingale if he did well on the circuit. He told me he used a lot of his inheritance from his mother to pay for all the expenses associated with showing the dog, figuring it would pay off in the long run. I'm sure that's why he wants to sue the pants off the homeowner's association."

"But wouldn't he have insurance on the dog?" she asked.

"Well, you know how it is. If insurance companies can blame someone else, they can refuse to pay. They probably told him it's up to us to make it right."

"And ours says it's up to his," Constance said. "Sounds typical."

"So tell us about Fulton," I said. "What kind of a guy is he? How do we best deal with him?"

"He's not a particularly nice guy," Garland said. "I think that's why he's a sutler instead of a soldier. He probably couldn't get along well with the rest of the unit."

"Not nice in what way?" Constance asked.

"He carries a chip on his shoulder all the time. It might have to do with his failure as a lawyer. I really don't know that much about him. But I make it a point to buy my goods from somebody else. Just don't want to deal with him."

"He doesn't sound like the kind of people I met in the reenactment," I said. "When I visited the encampment some years ago, everyone was so friendly and so eager to answer my questions. It seems like the point of it all is to share their knowledge and enthusiasm with the spectators."

"That's the whole idea," Garland said. "Fulton is an aberration."

I met Constance at her house on Saturday morning so we could go to Fulton's together. Joe said he would meet us there. We went a little early hoping to beat him, not knowing what would happen when these two combative men were in the same room. We hoped we could be a buffer between the two of them.

Fulton met us at the door, a man so thin he almost appeared skeletal. His bald dome was encircled by a longish fringe of dun-colored hair that hung over his jug-shaped ears in a failed attempt to hide them. A slight cast to his left eye drew attention to a hump in his nose which looked as though it had been broken and never set. He was a strange-looking duck. I wondered if that had something to do with his attitude. He ushered us into his living room without a word or a smile.

Dimly lit by one small table lamp, the drab room had a worn green faux leather sofa, a scratched maple coffee table and a huge television set that must have set him back a month's pay. In the corner was an empty dog cage, a half filled bowl of dog food and a bowl of water beside it, testament to the tragedy that had befallen Sir Martingale. I did feel bad about the dog's demise, a tragedy of course. But this man was taking advantage of the sad event to stick it to the homeowners' association.

"I'm Tommi Poag," I said offering my hand.

He ignored it, but turned to Constance and asked, "And you?"

"Constance Merritt," she replied, knowing better than to try and shake his hand. "I believe you know my husband Garland."

He wrinkled his brow for a moment then shook his head. "Don't think so."

"He's in the First Virginia Regiment at the reen-actments."

"Oh, yeah, one of the soldiers in fancy uniform. I guess I vaguely remember him."

He didn't offer to take our coats but indicated for

us to sit on the sofa and disappeared into the kitchen. I wondered if he was going to offer us refreshments, but he came back with a chrome dining chair which he plunked down facing away from us. He then straddled it and leaned his arms on the back. It was as if he was using the chair as a shield between us. Constance and I sat there getting warmer by the minute, but he took no notice of our discomfort. So we unzipped our jackets and sat with our hands in our pockets.

"So where's the other person?" he asked.

"We expect him at any minute," I replied.

Fulton looked at his watch with a disgruntled expression. It couldn't have been past ten o'clock yet. "Well, I wish he would get here. I haven't got all day. Can't we get this show on the road?"

"I think it best if we wait for Joe," Constance said.

His displeasure was obvious, and he continued to stare at us without another word. I was sure he was trying to put the whammy on us, get us psyched out before we even began our discussion. I wasn't going to let this twerp do his mental intimidation on me.

"Nice day out," I said blandly.

"If you say so," he replied.

Just then his doorbell rang. I didn't think I would welcome Joe's arrival, but at least it would break up this standoff. Of course things could get considerably worse as well.

Fulton answered the door and swung it wide, waving Joe into the room. Joe didn't even try to shake his hand but growled "Joe Kernodle," as he joined us on the sofa.

Constance and I decided the night before to start the meeting off on the right foot before Joe could alienate Fulton even more. She wasn't going to give him a chance to speak first.

So the minute he sat down, she turned to Fulton and said, "We're so sorry about your dog. We know it is a terrible tragedy for you."

"Damn right. Cost me a pretty penny." Not a tear shed over the dog himself, just the money he would have brought in.

"Yes," I said, "we understand he could have brought high stud fees." We had decided to acknowledge the fact that the dog could have made a lot of money rather than fight it. He could probably enlist experts to attest to the dog's worth.

"And his pups would sell for a bunch too," He answered. "Your damn painter has really wrecked all my plans. I put a ton of money into him." He was some kind of coldhearted SOB as far as I was concerned. He couldn't have cared less about poor Sir Martingale except for loss of future earnings. Not nearly as bad as people who sponsor dogfights of course, but I had a hunch that if the dog hadn't had a pedigree, he wouldn't have been past doing that.

"But a hundred thousand dollars," Joe said in his most contemptuous voice. "Let's get real here, Ridenhour."

Here we go, I thought.

Fulton gave him a blistering glare. "I spent almost all the money I got from Ma havin' that damn dog dragged around to all those shows, and I might as well as flushed it down the toilet. Do you know I've got ulcers from all this? I worried all the time the dog was on the show circuit whether or not he was gonna win because I had so much riding on him. After all that worrying, I thought I'd finally got to the point where I could cash in. And then some bloody bastard leaves his antifreeze out where any dog could get at it. I deserve to be reimbursed big time for all the grief I've been through."

Constance and I exchanged glances. This guy wasn't going to be amenable to compromise. But we had to try.

Constance spoke in soothing tones. "You know, sir, we just aren't going to be able to come up with the amount of money you are asking for."

"That's your problem."

"I don't think you understand what a serious situation this is for the homeowner's association. You are putting us in quite a bind."

Fulton looked at her with contempt. "Tough luck, lady."

"No," interceded Joe, "it's your tough luck, Ridenhour. You are going to make this suit go away."

Connie and I looked at him in shock. What did he think he was doing? This kind of tough talk wasn't going to work on this guy.

Fulton must have been thinking the same thing. "In

your dreams, Buddy. Don't go trying to push me around."

"Not my dreams," answered Joe. "This is your nightmare."

"What the hell are you talking about?" Fulton was really agitated now. Constance and I were totally out of the loop at this point and didn't have a clue what was happening.

I looked at her and she looked at me, and I could tell she felt as helpless as I did. Joe had finessed the discussion and left us on the sidelines.

Joe was looking smug now and full of himself. "I happen to have a friend who's a PI, and he owed me a favor. So I had him digging into your background."

I held my breath. I didn't like the way this conversation was going.

"Wait a minute, Joe," I said, "let's not…"

He waved me away. "Let me have my say here."

Fulton had a worried look in his eyes. I didn't know whether he knew what was coming or not. But he stuck out his chin as if to say "bring it on." He was full of bravado, the mantle often worn by pathetic men.

"I think you know what he found," Joe said with a malicious grin.

Fulton was looking decidedly uncomfortable now. He didn't seem to know whether to take a swing at Joe or to run away. Instead he just sat there mute.

"You came here from Missouri, didn't you?" It was like a cat playing with a mouse. Joe was enjoying watching Fulton squirm as he tweaked his tail slowly and methodically. "Kansas City, I believe, where you worked for the United Way."

Fulton's only answer was a savage glare.

"And it seems they came up a few thousand short on a campaign a few years ago."

"That's a lie!" Fulton hissed.

"Then how come they fired your ass?"

"That's none of your damn business, but it had nothing to do with taking money. Check it out with the police," Fulton was working up steam. "You won't find my name on any police blotter."

"No. I know that. That's because you groveled a lot, and they finally let you off when you promised to repay them. You were going to law school then, and you convinced them they would ruin your life if they brought charges. They really leaned over backward for you. In return you paid them in dribs and drabs until the statute of limitations to prosecute you ran out, and then you quit paying them altogether. That was a nice way to repay their kindness to you."

Fulton's mouth hung open. It was obvious he never expected this information to come to light. Finally he said, "So what? That's history."

"History that I think your employer might be very interested in."

Fulton got to his feet so fast he knocked the chair over backward, barely missing my feet. He lunged for Joe saying, "You bastard, I'll…"

Joe stood up and grabbed his arm, twisting it behind

Fulton's back. Joe probably weighed half again as much as his adversary, and he hardly broke a sweat. Fulton was bent over almost double. "Good thing I learned a little self defense back in the day. I could knock your lights out if I wanted to, but I don't pick on weaklings," Joe told him.

Constance and I had scrambled off the sofa as they grappled and scurried away from the confrontation to the corner of the room, not knowing what was going to happen next.

Joe forced Fulton to sit on the sofa before he released his arm and stood over him making sure he didn't get back up. Fulton's face was so dark I thought he was going to have a stroke. He was breathing heavily and clutching his knees so hard his fingernails could have cut right through the fabric. "You, you…," he snarled. He couldn't seem to find a word contemptuous enough to suit him.

"Now that I have your attention," Joe said, "I'd like to make a proposal. Drop the suit, and that little tidbit of information will go no further than this room. If you persist in it, you will be very, very sorry."

Constance and I just huddled in the corner. The situation was entirely out of our control.

Fulton took two or three deep breaths. "This is blackmail, pure and simple. I can't believe you would sink to this."

"I believe we are still miles higher than you, Buddy. You not only ripped off the United Way—*the United Way!*—" he made it sound like a sacrilege, which it

was "—you thought you could rip off the homeowners' association too. Well, I'm not gonna let you get
away with it. It was an accident, pure and simple, and
if you can't get relief from your own insurance, then
it's tough luck for you."

Joe turned to us. "I think it's time for the ladies and
me to leave. Don't bother getting up to show us out.
We can find our own way." He nodded toward the
door and said, "Let's go, ladies."

Fulton just sat there, his face getting stormier by the
minute. Not knowing what to say or do, I decided
leaving seemed the wisest choice before further
mayhem broke out. I put my arm around Constance's
shoulder and whispered in her ear, "I think we should."

She nodded and we hurried together to the door
followed by Joe. We waited till we were a block away
before we stopped and turned around to speak to him.

"What were you thinking!" Constance asked,
finally allowing her anger to show.

"You are really playing with fire," I added.

He grinned. "Can you think of a better way to
handle it? There was no way he was going to back
down otherwise."

"But," I argued, "we're representing a legal corporation. I don't see how we can deal with this in such
an unethical way."

"So you think corporations are always on the side
of the angels? That's a laugh. Besides, we were just
playing by his rules— he tried a little blackmail on us,

and we just turned the tables on him. What were you two planning to do?"

"Appeal to his good side. Make him see how devastating it would be for our association," Constance said.

Joe let out a belly laugh. "*Good side!* You've got to be kidding. That guy is nothing but a greedy, dishonest jackass who will take advantage of every situation he possibly can. There was no other way."

Neither of us said anything. In my heart I wondered if he was right.

FOUR

WE HAD TOLD RHONDA we would report to her as soon as our meeting with Fulton was over. I didn't know where she lived, but Constance had been to her house before. "It's two blocks over toward Lawndale," she said.

Joe started walking the other direction.

"Where are you going?" I asked.

"You gals can handle it. Tell her whatever you want. You can make up a story or tell her the truth, but I've done my bit."

"Joe," Constance said in a weary tone one would use on a disobedient child. She was shaking her head, her arms crossed over her chest in a gesture of disapproval. She looked like she wanted to turn him over her knee and give him a good spanking.

"Hey," he said, his palms upturned in a placatory gesture, "I said I'd help and I did. What more do you want?"

"Nothing," she said, dismissing him by turning her back and walking away. I hurried to catch up with her.

"Well, it looks like he left us to face the music," I said. "What do you think we should tell her?"

"Knowing Rhonda, she'll probably applaud his method. Somehow I find that very unappealing, having her cheer him on."

"Then why tell her? We could just say we managed to talk him out of it. Do we have to go into details?"

Constance thought about it for a minute or two. "I guess it would serve no purpose. The fewer people who know what happened, the better. It could get embarrassing if certain righteous people found out."

"Righteous people? What do you mean?"

"Oh, there are a couple of people on the board who have a pole up their you-know-what. If we step out of bounds even a little bit, they are all over us crying foul. And I usually agree with them, though I like to think I always consider all sides of the issue and try to be evenhanded. The fact is I'd be on their side in this case. But Joe caught us off guard, and now we're stuck with what he's done. I just don't want to make it any worse than it already is."

I felt a sense of relief. I really didn't want to have to explain how we let the situation get out of control.

Rhonda answered our knock and let us into her home. It was beautifully decorated with a taupe sectional sofa piled with colorful pillows facing a built-in bookcase wall that held a large flat screen TV set. What appeared to be hand-thrown vases and bowls graced the tables, and lovely watercolors hung on the walls. I hadn't expected her to have such good taste. Maybe subconsciously I just didn't want her to be good at anything. It's easier to write off people you don't like by deciding they have little or no talent. But I grudgingly admired her house and wished that mine could look half as good.

"Where's Joe?" she asked as we stood inside the front door in the entry way. She didn't ask us to sit down so apparently she had no intention of making a social visit out of it.

"He had something else he had to do," I hedged, imagining it was something like reading the morning paper or getting a latte at Starbucks.

"How did it go?" She had a hopeful look on her face. I wondered what her reaction might have been had we come back with bad news. Would she have gone ballistic? Would she have taken it calmly? I expected it would have been the former, and we probably would have gotten the blame. All along I was certain that she had handed off the responsibility of ensuring a good outcome to us so if it all went down the tubes, she could say it was our fault.

"It went well," Constance said without a hint of pre-varication in her voice. It happened that she was facing away from me, and I almost laughed when I noticed she had crossed the fingers on both hands behind her back.

I decided if she had to give a bald-faced lie, I should share in the guilt. "He agreed to back off very quickly," I said. "I don't think we have a thing to worry about any more." Actually, I could have passed a lie-detector test on that.

Rhonda beamed. "Well done, ladies! I must say

I'm surprised. I thought he would be a very tough nut to crack."

"People don't always react the way you anticipate," Constance said. "He turned out to be a sheep in wolf's clothing."

"Well, I know the Board will be thrilled. We should give you some kind of special recognition for handling it so successfully."

"Oh, please," I said, feeling guiltier by the minute, "don't do anything like that. We didn't do all that much. Really!"

"She's right," Constance added, "and I know Joe would agree."

I had to hide a grin at that. Joe was probably boasting to his buddies already that he had won the day for the condo association, although I prayed he would keep his promise to keep his mouth shut about the circumstances, at least in our neighborhood.

"Well, you're all too modest," Rhonda said.

We left before we had to lie any further and retreated to Constance's house.

"Stay for lunch," she urged me. "I don't know about you, but a glass of wine is in order. I wouldn't want to go through anything like that again. My nerves are pretty well shot."

"The wine sounds great. But I don't want you to go to any trouble."

"I've got some chicken salad from Fresh Market in the fridge. I'll toast some English muffins and cut up some fruit. No trouble at all."

When lunch was ready she called to Garland who was upstairs in the bedroom they'd converted into an office.

"How did the morning go?" he asked as he sat down to the dining table. "Did Fulton give you a hard time?"

We'd decided on the way to Constance's house to share the truth with Garland. We knew he wouldn't spread it any further. Above all we were hoping he would agree that we couldn't have done anything to stop the juggernaut that was Joe Kernodle.

"My God," he exclaimed after Constance had described our meeting blow by blow. "I know Joe only slightly, but I never liked him much. But this is pretty much over the top."

"What should we have done?" I asked.

"Sounds like your hands were tied. If he'd told you ahead of time, perhaps you could have talked him out of it, but I doubt it."

"We invited him to meet with us for a planning session, but he turned us down," Constance said. "He knew it would be much more effective by taking us all by surprise. Maybe stealth tactics are his natural way of doing things. What do you know about him, Garland?"

"He owns a printing company. I know that because his company prints the materials for the Guilford Courthouse reenactment."

"So you have connections with both Fulton and Joe," I said.

"Not really with Joe. Someone else handles all the

programs and such. I just happen to know who does it. I've heard them talk about how prickly he is to work with. In fact there has been some talk about changing printers just because he is so difficult."

"I can understand that," Constance said. "He doesn't exactly exude good vibes. I'd hate to do business with him."

"I think he has lost business because of his personality. Some people never learn that the customer is always right."

"When it comes to Joe," I said, "only Joe is right."

FIVE

RHONDA DIDN'T RECONVENE the board but sent all members a letter stating that the committee she appointed to handle the situation with Fulton Ridenhour had been successful and the suit had been dropped. I was enormously grateful that we hadn't been put in the position of describing our meeting with Fulton and having to answer questions. By the time we met again, I hoped that all we would encounter would be pats on the back and congratulatory handshakes. Even then I hoped I could refrain from looking sheepish, and that Joe would zipper his lip. Though I felt sure he wouldn't dare expose what he had done. That's the optimist in me.

It was mid-March and small signs of spring were beginning to appear. The forsythia had come and gone, and tulips and daffodils were now in evidence. I could make out tiny buds on the dogwood and redbud trees, and the Bradford pears, cherry trees and other early bloomers were on the verge of busting out all over. I don't think there's anywhere on earth more beautiful than Greensboro in the spring. The dogwood is so prevalent one would think when it blooms that the town had been surprised by a late snowstorm for the streets are lined with white. And the yards are blessed with mounds of azaleas covering the spectrum from pale pink to bright red to light lavender. But the height of bloom would be mid-April. Most of the trees were still barren now and a winter chill still held us captive.

Garland called me one evening to tell me the reen-actment of the Battle of Guilford Courthouse would be held that weekend.

"I wanted to personally invite you to come this Sunday," he said. "If you could come around 12:30 or so I can show you around the encampment. The battle starts at two. Constance will take you over there, but she's out at some meeting tonight so I thought I'd give you a call."

"I thought she wasn't all that interested in it."

"She just doesn't want to do all the work involved in putting it together. She does like to watch."

"I'd love to, Garland. You really intrigued me with some of your tales."

CONSTANCE AND I LEFT at noon on Sunday to drive to Price Park where the reenactment was held. She was driving her big Dodge SUV and complaining about the cost of gas and how her car seemed to slurp it up. "We wanted to trade it in, but they won't give us enough for it to cover the cost of our loan, so we're stuck with it."

"Why on earth didn't you let me drive then?" I asked. I had splurged a few months earlier and turned in my old car for a new Honda Fit, a little five-door cross between a wagon and small SUV. It was cute as a button and got great gas mileage, although it was a struggle to make the payments on my salary. But I wasn't sorry.

"Because I invited you," she said. "And it really isn't that far. I was just venting."

"Aren't we all," I said. "We could have walked if they still held it at Battleground Park. Why did they move it?"

"There isn't enough space. Price Park has a big open field that's much more suited to it. They do have some of the encampments and the field hospital set up at Battleground Park and many demonstrations. There are craftsmen and sutlers over at Price Park and the British soldiers are camping out at Tannenbaum Historic Park. You know where that is, don't you?"

"Sure, next to the Battleground Park on New Garden Road."

"Right. That was bought by private donations some years ago, because it served as a staging area for the British troops. The old house there belonged to a long-ago county sheriff."

"You might claim not to be all that interested, but I can tell you've picked up a lot of information," I said.

"I can't help it. When your mate is so caught up in something, it rubs off on you. I'm not as disinterested as he likes to claim. He just thinks I am because I don't want to sleep on the ground in some damned pup tent and eat beans cooked over an open fire."

"Well, I'm sure it's a major commitment."

"You bet your booties it is. Ah, here we are."

She was turning off New Garden Road onto Jefferson Club Road which led into the park and on up the hill to the Kathleen Clay Edwards branch library. At the foot of the hill a number of small white tents stood in rows and a bevy of "soldiers," some dressed in colorful jackets with white breeches and others in white tunics and pants, milled about checking muskets and looking over a cannon. Garland had told me the white tunics were the common garb for hunters and that Washington had wanted his army to be clothed this way because the British would assume the men were marksmen. It was also far less expensive. But Congress overrode him, wanting their army to wear European style uniforms. In spite of that, the hunters' frock was frequently used by many in North Carolina who could not afford the expensive wool to make the uniforms.

Constance found a parking spot on the berm, and we followed a gravel road on foot a few hundred feet to a larger area where the sutlers' tents, much larger than those for the soldiers, stood in a row in the field.

Constance spotted Garland talking to several men standing by another cannon and we joined them. As I had envisioned, Garland looked smashing in his uniform: blue coat with red trim down the front and at the cuffs with rows of pewter buttons. A wide white band across one shoulder held his canteen at his back, and white breeches topped dark gaiters. A ruffle at his throat and the tricorn hat added extra dash as did a burgundy sash around his waist. A short sword hung at his side. Garland had told me earlier that he'd bought it from an on-line firm called Noblewares, and it was the exact duplicate of a sword used by officers at the battle of Guilford Courthouse.

"There you are," Garland greeted us with a smile. "Connie, you know these guys."

She nodded her head. "Good to see you all."

"And Tommi, this is George Jennings, Jeff Lambert, and Stuart Steele," he said, indicating the men from left to right.

I shook hands with all of them. I took delight to note that all of the men looked pretty spectacular in their uniforms. It was if by becoming Revolutionary soldiers, they had morphed into rare creatures.

I noticed a crescent-shaped silver ornament hanging on a ribbon around Garland's neck. "What's that?" I asked.

"That's called a gorget. It's supposed to represent the last vestige of armor and shows I'm a commissioned officer."

"Instead of bars on your shoulders, I guess."

"Yes, they fell out of favor after the Revolutionary war. What do you say we take a tour of the sutlers' tents," Garland suggested. He led us up the rise to one that featured weapons such as rifles and pistols, bayonets and swords, and finished clothing for men and women. When I checked the price tags of a couple of jackets I understood why Garland made his own.

A burly man was rearranging some of his wares. A bushy gray beard and shoulder-length hair framed a face that belonged on a backwoodsman, rugged and darkly tanned. He was wearing a loose fitting shirt and baggy pants that looked as though they'd been around for two hundred years.

"Hi, Steve," Garland said. "How's it going?"

The men shook hands. "You know my wife Connie, don't you?" he said.

"Sure. Good to see you," Steve made a courtly little bow.

"And this is our friend, Tommi Poag. She's new to the experience. Steve Leonard."

He smiled at me. "Welcome to the eighteenth century. Sometimes it's good to get away from the twenty-first for a little while. I, for one, could do without cell phones and Internet and all the rest of the modern world. Well, at least on weekends," he amended.

Okay, I thought, it does have its drawbacks at times, but I'm not sure I'd want to give them all up. But to be polite I said, "I know what you mean."

Steve showed us around his "shop" and explained how some of the more arcane items were used.

"Well, we need to get on if they're going to see the rest of the sutlers," Garland finally said. I had the feeling Steve would gladly spend the afternoon talking about his wares if we let him.

We continued down the row. Each tent held items necessary for an authentic experience from the proper buttons and trims, to big brimmed hats that could be made into tricorns by pulling strings threaded through the brim. Everything you could think of related to the life of an eighteenth century soldier and his family was available in one of the portable "shops."

"The next tent is where Fulton Ridenhour sells his fabric. Do you two want to go in there or skip it?" Garland asked us.

Constance and I looked at each other. "What do you think, Tommi?" she asked.

"I'm curious," I said. "We can't avoid him forever since he lives in our neighborhood. I can't imagine he would make a scene here."

"Okay. Let's check it out," Constance said.

Garland led the way into the tent. Tables lining the back and the sides were piled with bolts of blue and red wool, white linen and flax fabrics for breeches and tunics, and fabrics suitable for women's clothes. Fulton was talking to a man dressed in hunter's clothes with a fluffy sheepskin backpack hanging from his shoulders.

When the man left, he turned to us with a smile that quickly faded when he recognized us.

"Did you come to harass me?" he growled. His eyes looked a little wild and he had backed up against a table as if we were going to attack him.

"Of course not, Fulton," I assured him. "We were just interested in what you had to sell here."

"Don't worry. I'm all square with the IRS if that's what you're thinking."

"Come on now," Constance said. "That incident

the other day is over. We aren't going to bother you any more. We're just here for the reenactment."

"Says who? Can you vouch for Joe Kernodle? He'll probably be on my case for the rest of my life."

"No he won't," I said, although I couldn't really be sure. "I think you should know that Constance and I had nothing to do with his actions. We didn't know what was going to happen." I hadn't meant to say that, but I suddenly felt the need to proclaim my innocence.

Constance threw me a sharp glance as if to warn me to keep my mouth shut.

"That's a laugh," Fulton said bitterly. "I know you were all in this together. You'll be sorry someday."

"That's enough, Fulton," Garland said sharply. "We didn't come in here so you could threaten these ladies." He gestured to Constance and me. "Come on, let's get out of here."

We walked hurriedly toward the other side of the encampment where a meal was being cooked over an open fire.

"That man is a nut case," Constance said as we stopped to watch a woman and young boy tend a pot that contained some kind of stew. Three five-foot-long poles formed a sort of teepee over the fire, and the pot dangled from a chain in the center. The woman kept a sharp eye on the boy as he stirred the contents with a long spoon, making sure he didn't get too close to the fire.

"He's a dangerous man," Garland said. "I think you should steer clear of him."

"Damn Joe Kernodle," I added. "He put us in this

position. Though I think Fulton is all bluff. He doesn't impress me as the kind who would physically harm someone."

"I wouldn't be so sure," Garland said. "Joe, in effect, raised doubts about his manhood when he got the better of him. Guys like Fulton don't take kindly to any suggestion that they are unmanly and have to prove that they're tough."

At that moment George Jennings, whom we met over by the cannon, walked up and joined us.

"Are you enjoying the tour, ladies?" he asked.

"With one exception," I answered.

He looked at Garland questioningly.

"Oh, we had a little run-in with Fulton Ridenhour."

George snorted. "Little pipsqueak. Like half the world hasn't had some kind of confrontation with him. Do you know he shorted me on material that I bought for my regimental jacket? I paid for the full yardage, but when I went to cut it out, I didn't have enough for one of the sleeves. That wool is damned expensive too. When I confronted him about it, he called me a liar, and said I could never prove it."

"I'm surprised they let him continue to be part of this reenactment," I said.

"He may not be much longer. If any more complaints are made against him, I think he'll be out on his ass."

George's cheeks colored. "Sorry, ladies, that's eighteenth century speak you know."

Garland roared. "Sure, George, sure."

We wandered around a bit before Garland told us it was time for the troops to assemble.

"Let me show you a good spot to watch the battle," he said, leading us over to the area that had been cordoned off with yellow tape. "This little rise here gives you a good view. Did you bring ear plugs, Tommi?"

"I did. Constance warned me about the noise."

"Well, I've got some things that need attending to before the battle starts, so I've got to go."

He and Constance kissed goodbye and he left.

People were beginning to assemble around the perimeter of the battlefield though it was still about twenty minutes before it would start. While Constance and I were chatting, I felt someone tap me on the shoulder. I turned around to see Mack Thurston, a member of our condo association board.

"Hi, ladies," he said.

We both nodded hello.

"Your husband is one of the reenactors, isn't he?" he asked Constance.

"He is," she said. "Been doing it for some time now. Do you come to this every year?"

"Last year was the first time. I got interested in it because of the Greensboro Bicentennial. They had so much going on for the celebration, and I thought I should learn more about local history. They put on quite a show here, don't they?"

"They do indeed," she said.

"I understand that you two and Joe talked Ridenhour out of suing us. How'd you do that? I know he's one hard case."

Oh, Lord, I was afraid this was going to happen some day. I could see by the look in Constance's eyes that she was trying to come up with some innocuous answer, but hadn't yet devised one. I took a stab at it.

"I guess we just caught him at a weak moment. He was surprisingly flexible," I said. Oh, yes, Joe managed to twist his arm very easily. It really wasn't a lie.

I looked at Constance, and she was having a difficult time trying to keep a straight face. "That's right," she said, "he caved in right away."

"Can't imagine," Mack said. "You know, I live a couple of doors down from him."

"No, I didn't," I said.

"Yeah, it was the guy between us who left out the antifreeze. I thought Fulton was going to kill him. Bob had to take out a restraining order. But when you live right next door, he's hard to avoid. Bob has put his home on the market to get away from him."

"Wow," Constance said, "in this market? He'll have a hard time. Not much is selling now."

"I know. That makes it worse. And I have a history with the guy as well. I was glad Rhonda didn't ask me to be on the committee to meet with him 'cause I probably would have punched him out."

Join the crowd I thought. "What did he do to you?" I asked.

"Every time he walked the dog, he'd let it do his

business in my yard. I got damned tired of cleaning up after him. And the dog would raise his leg on my bushes which killed them. I know Ridenhour did it deliberately. He loves to torment people."

"Did you say anything to him?" Constance asked.

"Many times over. He'd just sneer at me and say, 'He's gotta do it somewhere.'"

Our conversation was interrupted by a thunderous explosion. We turned to see smoke pouring from a cannon at the far edge of the field and troops lined up at both ends, the British in their scarlet coats on one side, Americans in blue as well as the men dressed as hunters at the other, muskets raised and poised to fire. I quickly searched in my purse for my earplugs. A cannon from the opposite end belched smoke as it erupted in another deafening blast.

As the British began to advance, the Americans opened fire with their muskets, a series of popping sounds that spewed smoke which briefly covered the field, obscuring the combatants. Some of the men in the British forward line fell to the ground as if dead or wounded. It was almost too lifelike for me. At least they didn't try to replicate bleeding wounds or I probably would have left. I'm a real coward when it comes to even small amounts of gore.

The British troops then regrouped and stepped over their men who had fallen and continued to advance forward, finally stopping and firing their own guns into the American line which quickly fell apart. The North Carolina militia, in the front, retreated, leaving their stricken fellow soldiers lying in the field. They moved around and behind the second line of General Greene's troops.

I turned to Constance. "I had no idea how realistic this would be. The only thing lacking is the blood."

"They've done it so many times it's like a choreographed dance. They know just where to go and what to do."

The battle continued on with cannons blasting, muskets firing, and men falling to the ground in the throes of mock death. At one moment it seemed the red coats were winning; at other times the American troops were apparently on top.

Soon the soldiers were engaged in hand-to-hand battle. There was a great roiling mass of soldiers, some in red, some in blue, others all in white, grappling with one another while the sun glinted off of steel bayonets and swords.

"My God!" I exclaimed to Constance. "Isn't that dangerous? Won't someone get hurt with all those blades being thrown about?"

Constance smiled. "It looks real, doesn't it? As I said it's like a dance. The guys raise their bayonets and swords into the air so it gives the illusion of a desperate fight. When they're in such a crowd, it looks like they're engaging in battle from a distance. But, believe me, they've done it many times before and nobody gets hurt."

"Scares the heck out of me," I said.

After this attack, Greene ordered a full retreat. As

history shows, although Cornwallis won this battle, he lost so many troops that it turned the tide of the war, and he surrendered at Yorktown within months of the Battle of Guilford Courthouse. When the reenactment was over, an eerie silence fell over the crowd. Although it had all been make-believe, it seemed so authentic we were reminded of the sacrifices so many good men have made throughout the centuries to make and keep our country free.

Eventually the spectators began to stir and move away.

"I told Garland we'd go on home," Constance said. "He'll be here until after five, but I didn't think we needed to stay till then."

"Fine by me," I said. My ears were still ringing from the cannon fire despite my ear plugs, and the experience, while exhilarating, had taken an emotional toll. I was ready to leave.

We were walking back through the encampment when we heard a blood curdling scream from the direction of the sutlers' tents. A woman dressed in colonial garb dashed out of Fulton Ridenhour's tent yelling, "Oh, my God! Someone's dead in there!" For a moment I wondered if this was part of the reenactment before realizing that the "killing" had been confined to the battlefield. This had to be real!

Constance grabbed my arm. "Let me see if I can help," she said. "Maybe the person is just unconscious."

"I'm with you," I said. "Lead the way."

People had stopped in their tracks, unsure of what

to do. A few either wanting to help or merely curious hurried toward Fulton's tent.

By the time we arrived, several spectators and a couple of reenactors stood around someone crumpled on the ground beside a table covered with bolts of cloth. I couldn't see the face, but the man was clothed in a costume similar to what Fulton was wearing. I was so startled, I was unable to react for a moment. No one else seemed to know what to do either until Constance brushed aside two onlookers and knelt next to the body, her nursing instincts taking over. She felt the carotid artery, looked up at me and shook her head and formed the words silently, "He's been killed."

The realization that someone had actually died snapped me back into action.

"Has anyone called 911?" I asked.

The woman who had found him held out her cell phone. "I did," she said. I wondered where on earth in her colonial costume she carried it and how ludicrous it seemed for her to be holding it.

"Call them back and tell them to send the police as well as the emergency squad. This could be a crime scene, and we don't want to compromise it. Is there a way we can block off this tent so no one goes in until the police get here?" I began shooing the spectators back out into the center of the circle of tents.

One of the sutlers spoke up. "I have some cord in my tent. We can pound in some stakes by the front corners of the tent and tie the cord between them."

"I saw some branches by one of the fires," I said. "I can break them in pieces for stakes." I hurried over to the fire where I'd seen the child and his mother preparing a meal earlier, and picked up a couple of sticks from their firewood. Someone found a hammer, and together we pounded short pieces of wood into the ground outside of Fulton's tent and tied the cord furnished by the sutler to each one. It wasn't as good as a yellow crime scene tape, but it served the purpose in a pinch.

No one seemed ready to leave. The air was filled with murmurs as the crowd grew and the speculation mounted. We had seen dozens of men in poses of the dead and dying, and it seemed impossible that someone died for real now.

I spoke softly to Constance so no one else could hear. "What makes you think there's been a crime? Couldn't it have been a heart attack or something?"

"Because when I leaned over him, I saw blood underneath him. You couldn't see it because it was between him and the table."

Thank the Lord I wasn't the one who had seen it or I probably would have fainted on top of him. "Was it Fulton for sure?"

"Yeah, though I couldn't get a real good look at his face, I remembered seeing the scar on his neck from carotid artery surgery the day we were at his house. I guess I notice those things having been a nurse."

"I didn't like the guy, and apparently a lot of other people didn't either. But I can't believe someone would kill him."

"Me either," Constance said. "But there may be a

lot we don't know about Fulton. Who knows what sort of crazy things he might have pulled on others?"

The emergency squad arrived first followed by two police cars a short time later. The EMS, after confirming he was dead, stood waiting at the tent's entrance until the police arrived. After conferring with them, the police radioed for the crime scene unit and asked the crowd to gather at the other end of the encampment and not to leave the site. Some of the officers spread out to round up everyone in the area. Since the reenactors were all still there as well as the camp followers and the spectators who hadn't yet left, there ended up being quite a crowd of people the police wanted to question.

A harsh wind had begun to blow and the sky was clouding up.

"How long do you think they are going to keep us?" Constance asked me. "I'm freezing just standing here."

"As long as they please," I said. "I don't think they really care if we get pneumonia or not."

Garland came over to us. "What's going on?" he asked. "The cops wouldn't tell us why they were herding us all over here."

"It looks like Fulton might have gotten himself killed," Constance answered.

"You're joking! How?"

"We don't know," Constance said. "Someone found him in his tent. I was one of the first there, and I checked his carotid. He was gone. And I saw some blood underneath him. But I've no idea what happened."

Garland just shook his head. "It's getting pretty cold to be standing around like this. Wonder if they'd let us light up some of the camp fires."

One of the cops stepped forward and indicated he wanted quiet. It took a while for the whole crowd to realize he was signaling for them to stop talking. When he finally got silence he said, "We've made arrangements for all of you to walk up the hill to the library. We've cleared out the patrons and librarians, and there will be plenty of chairs for all and restrooms and water fountains. We want to talk to all of you so it might take a while. We'll try to make you as comfortable as possible."

"I think it's going to be a long night," I said.

SIX

AND A LONG NIGHT IT WAS. Constance and I were questioned fairly early on since we were among the first people to arrive at the scene. It was around 5:30 when we were told we could leave. We'd been sitting in the children's room at the Kathleen Clay Edwards library with Garland, speculating on what had happened. It seemed rather unholy to be talking about a possible homicide next to a winsome mural depicting charming animals in a woodland glade.

"Why do you think someone would kill him here?" I asked. "It seems like a strange place to commit murder."

"Not really," Garland said. "There's safety in numbers you know, and with such a crowd here, it would be easy to blend in with everyone else."

"But weren't there usually people in his tent?"

"When the battle reenactment starts, everyone heads over to the field to watch it. That would be the perfect time to do it."

There wasn't much I could tell the cop who questioned me. I described how Constance and I had gone to the tent where Fulton lay after we heard the woman scream. I told him that Constance had checked on him because of her nurse's training and then, sensing that is was a crime scene, I suggested that the tent be cordoned off.

"And what made you think it was a crime scene?" he asked. He'd told me his name was Detective Arnold, and he was with CID. He was a young man, small in stature, who looked more like a college student than a cop. But he more than made up for his youth by his commanding presence. Though he was perfectly polite to us, I could see where he could intimidate a criminal. I wondered if this was one of his first murder cases and he was anxious to make a good impression on his superiors.

"When my friend checked his carotid artery, she could see that there was blood underneath him that wasn't evident to the rest of us."

"Did you touch anything around him?" he asked.

"No, of course not," I said.

He smiled a knowing smile. "A fan of Law and Order, I would guess."

"My favorite show. I watch the reruns all the time."

"So do lots of people. Makes them think they can solve crimes." He said this with a bit of a smile as if he were thinking that this "little old lady" must think she's Miss Marple. I didn't think it wise to tell him I actually had solved a couple of murders in my time. Somehow I tend to be in the wrong place at the wrong time or perhaps the right place if one's mind runs to that sort of thing. It's just that friends or acquaintances get themselves in nasty situations, and I can't bear to stand by and see them accused of something I know they couldn't have done.

Another cop was interviewing Constance at the same time. When we were done we went back to where we'd been sitting with Garland.

"You two go on home. No sense in waiting around for me since you have your own car. God knows when they'll get around to the reenactors. They seem to be interviewing the spectators first."

"That's because all you guys were still over in the field," Constance said. "Someone in the encampment area is more likely to have done it. In fact, he, she, whoever, probably did it when everyone was watching the battle and is long gone by now."

"That's true," I said. "But you know the cops have to go through the paces. No matter how inconvenient it is for everyone."

Garland wouldn't hear of us staying around to keep him company, so we finally gave in and drove toward home.

"Let me treat you to supper," I said. "I don't feel like fixing anything, and I'm sure you don't either."

"Okay," she said. "Where to?"

"How about Village Tavern? Since it's pretty early yet, maybe it won't be too crowded."

She drove to the perennially popular restaurant at the corner of Battleground and Westridge Roads. We took a seat in the bar which was a little quieter than the main dining room and ordered wine and crab cakes, their specialty.

Once we were served we began to discuss the death of Fulton Ridenhour.

"Do you have any idea how he was killed?" I asked Constance.

"I'd say either he was shot or stabbed."

"What makes you say that?"

"There was quite a bit of blood which you couldn't see, and some had spread underneath the table but was hidden by the tablecloth. It seemed to come from his midsection. If he'd been shot, the noise would have blended in with the noise of the battle. So it's really hard to say."

"Is there anything we know about him that would lead someone to murder?" I couldn't help myself. The puzzle connected to something like this always intrigued me. The kinds of killings one reads about in the paper every day related to drug dealing or robbery were cut and dried. No mystery there. Even those between battling spouses or lovers were pretty easy to figure out. But Fulton lived alone, and if he had a relationship with a woman, we didn't know about it. I couldn't imagine that he had enough money on hand at the reenactment that someone would rob him. At least it seemed like an unlikely place for a petty thief. And surely it wouldn't have been the place for a drug deal gone wrong. So who would have wanted Fulton dead?

"We've heard several people in our neighborhood gripe about Fulton for one thing or another. I guess the worst was the way he tried to hold up the condo association for the death of his dog. But that was settled, thanks to Joe, so none of the homeowners could be upset about that," Constance said.

I agreed. "Good old Joe. I think Fulton would have wanted to kill him, not the other way around."

"Mack Thurston from our board said Fulton let his dog do his business in his yard all the time."

"I can't believe that would have led him to murder. Dog poop doesn't seem like much of a motive. Nor would I suspect George Jennings who said Fulton cheated him on the yard goods he bought from him."

"Yeah, you're right. Fulton has done things to annoy many people, but I don't see any reason for murder there."

"But how about that Bob somebody-or-other Mack was telling us about? Remember he lives, whoops that's wrong, *lived* next door to Fulton and was the one who left out the antifreeze. Mack said he had to take out a restraining order on Fulton. He's been trying to sell his house, but in this market he's probably stuck with it. Maybe he was so afraid of Fulton he decided to get rid of the guy before Fulton could harm him."

"That's a pretty interesting theory," Constance agreed. "Do you think we ought to tell the cops?"

"I think they'll find it out for themselves. They're bound to interview the neighbors."

Although we couldn't come up with any other possible suspects, we continued to talk about the events of the day throughout our dinner.

Finally Constance said, "Garland is sure to be starved when he gets home. I should get back so I can get something together for him."

She dropped me off at my house, and I turned on Channel 14 that runs local news twenty-four hours a day to see if Fulton's death was being reported yet.

They had distant shots of the abandoned camp site with patrol cars and a crime scene van parked nearby and exterior shots of the library where they said participants and spectators were being questioned in the death of one of the merchants who sold wares during the encampment. They had very few details, not even the name of the deceased because next-of-kin had not yet been notified. It made me wonder who Fulton's next-of-kin were.

I WAS ALREADY IN BED when the phone rang. It was Constance.

"They've got Garland in custody!" she cried. Normally she was the most self-assured and in-control person I knew, but her voice betrayed shock and disbelief.

"They've got him in custody?" I was in denial. How could that be?

"They think he had something to do with Fulton's death."

"That's the most absurd thing I ever heard. Why would they think that?"

"I don't know. But he called me from jail. He wants

me to find a lawyer so he can get bailed out. Isn't your ex a lawyer?"

"He's not a criminal lawyer, Constance. You need someone who is."

"But didn't you tell me he used to be in the public defender's office, and he represented your friend when she was accused of killing her husband?"

"Well, yes. But I wasn't happy about that because it had been so many years since he'd handled criminal cases."

"But she got off, didn't she?"

"That was because I discovered the real murderer. It never went to trial."

"I also recall you told me he won some big cases when he was a public defender. What if your ex agreed to let you help him investigate? You two could work together. Didn't you tell me you solved another murder as well? The one that happened at the Girl Scout camp? We really need you on our side. Please, Tommi, I don't know where else to turn."

"Bernard handled those cases years ago. Honestly, Constance, I think you need a bona fide defense lawyer."

"Would another attorney let you work with him?"

"Probably not."

"Please, Tommi. Please at least ask him. If he says no, I'll try to find someone else. Do this for me." Her tone was so pleading I finally gave in.

"I'll call him," I said. "But I'm sure he'll refuse."

Bernard is something of a night owl, unlike me

who always hits the sheets well before the late night talk shows, so I knew he would still be up.

When he answered the phone, he growled, "Yes?" He was probably watching TV and didn't want to be interrupted.

"It's me, Tommi."

"Kind of late for you, isn't it?" It used to irk him when I turned in so early. I kept trying to tell him that I couldn't fight my body rhythms, but he said that was nonsense.

"I have a favor to ask you."

"Why is it you always want favors late at night? Do you think that I'm more amenable then and more likely to say yes?"

I laughed, something I couldn't have done two years earlier. "Don't forget I lived with you for thirty-three years. I know better than that."

"Well, get on with it. I'm trying to watch *BC World*."

I thought so. "I have a friend whose husband is in jail suspected of murder. She called me just now almost in hysterics. Wants someone to get him out on bond."

"Not again, Tommi. How in hell do you get involved in such things?"

"I seem to remember it was because of you I got involved before. Just to refresh your memory, when your cousin's daughter was arrested, I was the one who begged you *not* to take the case if you'll recall. But you persisted. And the next time I was the one who saved your sorry butt when the cops thought you'd killed Evan." Evan had been my divorce lawyer, and he was shot during a Girl Scout disaster exercise at their camp. "So I think you owe me big time, Bernard."

"I suppose I do." He sounded almost sheepish now. That was a first.

"Suppose? I'm sure you can do better than that!"

"Oh, come on, Tommi, don't give me a hard time. Just tell me about it."

"Garland Merritt is a history teacher who lives in my complex. His wife and I are on the association board together."

"You mean they conned you into that? You're the perennial sucker, Tommi."

He was right, but it made me mad for him to say so. "Somebody's got to do it, Bernard. Anyway, that's neither here nor there. Let's talk about Garland."

"Go ahead. I'll keep my mouth shut."

That would be a first. "Garland is a reenactor, and today he took part in the reenactment of the Battle of Guilford Courthouse over in Price Park."

"I've never been to it."

"Well, you should go. It's fascinating. And you learn a lot of local history."

"So how did he end up in jail?"

"When the battle was over, someone found one of the sutlers dead…"

"One of the what?"

"Sutlers. They're the ones who sell all the goods they need to make their costumes or firearms or cookware since they camp out for the weekend and cook over open fires. That sort of thing."

"You mean salesmen. Why didn't you just say so?"

"Because they called them sutlers in the eighteenth century, and these people are authentic to the nth degree."

"So how was this sutler or whatever killed?"

"I don't know. Garland's wife Constance is a nurse, and since she and I were nearby when someone discovered the body, she checked his carotid. She saw a lot of blood under him so she thinks he was either shot or stabbed."

"What do the cops say?"

"As far as I know they haven't said anything."

"And why do they suspect your friend?"

"I haven't a clue. He would seem to be the last person I'd suspect of doing it. So are you going to help them?"

"Well, at least I'll go bail him out. I want to talk to him before I decide."

"I guess that's fair enough. I told Constance I wasn't at all sure you would do it. But she's pretty frantic, so if you could help them tonight, I'd be forever grateful."

SEVEN

I WENT BACK TO BED but it was impossible to sleep. I didn't usually let Tee sleep with me at night, but I lured him into bed with treats just to have his warm body next to mine to comfort me. I'm afraid I started something because now he isn't happy unless I let him curl up on top of the blankets every night. But he's so quiet I should have done that long ago. Considering he saved my life a couple of years ago when my condo was on fire, I should let him do anything he wants. He's Top Cat in my book.

I went to work the next morning feeling hung over from lack of sleep. I must have looked it too, because Logan Stahl, my boss, greeted me with, "You look bushed. Didn't you get your usual beauty rest last night?"

He and I make up the office staff at Stewardship Life in a fifty-year-old building on Eugene Street. I had not worked during my marriage to Bernard, and armed with only a degree in Liberal Arts from prehistoric times, I really wasn't prepared for much of anything except laundry, house cleaning, and the fine art of shopping. Even the fact I had one year of law school only to drop out to marry Bernard and put *him* through law school didn't add much to my sketchy resume. So I've always been grateful to Logan for hiring me.

He offered me one of the Krispy Kreme donuts he buys daily to go with our morning coffee. The only reason he manages to keep a trim waistline at age sixty-one is because he spends weekends on the golf course. I don't think he has broken eighty yet, but he never gives up. "This should get you going," he said. I, as always, thanked him but refused. Since I don't golf or do much else in the way of exercise, I'd be a blimp by now if I ever indulged. That is my solitary concession to dieting.

He sat in his chair chewing thoughtfully, running his fingers through his auburn hair, now touched with gray, that curls over the edges of his small, neat ears and the collar of his dress shirt. It amazes me that he doesn't keep it cut more conservatively since he spends so much time out selling policies. But it doesn't seem to affect his sales. Apparently his jovial personality makes up for that small lapse. I think it was his one nod to mid-life angst, and he's kept it long ever since.

"Didn't I hear on the morning news that someone in your neighborhood was murdered yesterday?"

"I'm afraid so. That's why I didn't get any sleep. A friend was arrested for it."

He shook his head in disbelief. "I don't know what

it is about you, Tommi. You're a magnet for trouble. And you seem like such a guileless lady!"

"I know. It scares me. I'm afraid to make friends anymore for fear they'll be accused of something terrible."

"Did you know the victim as well? I understand he lived near you too."

"I did. In fact about two weeks ago I had a run-in with him." I went on to tell Logan the whole story about Fulton and the lawsuit.

"So the wife of the guy who was arrested was with you when all this happened."

"Right."

"Do you think there's some connection?"

"I can't see how. Joe was the one who threatened to reveal his embezzling. Fulton had no beef with us, though he thought we were in on it. He was a little threatening when we saw him Sunday at the reenactment, but we weren't frightened by it. And I can't believe Garland is the kind of person who would kill anyone."

"It seems to me I've heard you say that before."

"Yeah, and I was proved right, wasn't I? I think I'm a pretty good judge of character."

"It's too bad the cops don't ask your opinion before they arrest somebody," Logan said.

CONSTANCE CALLED ME as soon as I got home from work. I'd tried reaching her a couple of times during the day, but I got no answer. "Can I come over and talk to you?" she asked.

"Don't you know I've been dying to hear from you? I'll open a bottle of wine." I don't often drink wine at home, but I thought we both could use a glass.

She was there within ten minutes. She sat in my bentwood rocker looking wan and tired. Tee had curled up on her lap, and she was stroking his back. There's nothing like petting a cat to calm one's anxieties. Almost as good as a shrink.

I brought her a glass a white zin, the only thing I had on hand.

"So where's Garland?" I asked.

"He's at school gathering up his stuff. They asked him not to come back till this thing is resolved."

"Whatever happened to the presumption of innocence?"

"They were afraid it would be too disruptive, that the students would be thinking about the murder and not about their lessons."

"That sucks! So what's going on? Why on earth would the cops think Garland did it? That's the craziest thing I've ever heard."

"It seems that Fulton was stabbed."

"You'd said that you thought he might have been. So why would they think Garland did it?"

"They found blood on his sword."

"Good Lord! Didn't he notice it?"

"It had apparently been wiped off. But not well enough. The cops found dried blood around the handle. Garland never saw it. You know how they wave them in the air during the reenactment then stick them back in the scabbard so he never looked at it closely."

"Well, that's pretty scary. How could someone else have used it?"

"You remember those tall bushes just behind the encampment?"

"I guess so. Didn't pay much attention."

"They had some Porta Jons back there. Since the reenactors spend the whole weekend out on that hill, they need to have facilities."

"Okay." I couldn't imagine where this was going.

"Just before Garland went over to the field for the battle, he had to use one. Those things are small, and it's hard to get into one with your sword and all. It's hard enough to get those buttoned-up trousers down. So he laid the sword on the ground beside the Jon. Fulton's tent was very close, just on the other side of the bushes. Someone could have taken it, stabbed Fulton, wiped it off, and had it back in the scabbard in a matter of minutes."

"Didn't he tell the cops that?"

"Of course. But they thought it was too far-fetched. Said only his fingerprints were on it."

"Well, duh, the perp could have used gloves."

"I know. There's got to be something else going on we don't know about."

"Oh, Constance, I'm so sorry. What a mess. What about Bernard? Did he agree to take the case?"

"He said he'd let us know by tonight."

BERNARD CALLED ME before I heard from Constance.

"I've decided to take your friend's case," he said without preamble.

"I'm surprised. I didn't really expect you to. I thought you didn't want to do defense work any more."

"I didn't want to stay with the Public Defender's office because it didn't pay squat. But I'll have to admit that winning criminal cases is something of an ego trip."

I gritted my teeth to keep from saying what I wanted to say, that it was always about Bernard, not about the defendant.

"But what about your firm? I didn't think they handled that sort of thing."

"They've decided to expand. In these lean times some of our corporate work has fallen off as of course real estate business has, so they need to branch out. Since I've had experience along those lines, they decided I should take the case."

"Well, I'll be damned."

"And I've decided I want you to work for me."

This really blew my mind. When his cousin's daughter Nina was arrested for murdering her husband, I begged him to let me help but he flat out refused. And he wasn't even gracious about it. I had to investigate behind his back. That was the only criminal case he'd been involved in for years, and he took that only because he'd been close to Nina and she wanted him to represent her.

"What can I say? This is certainly an about-face in your attitude."

"I know, I know. But you did get me off the hook when they thought I'd murdered Evan. That was a nice piece of work."

Bernard, praising me? I couldn't believe it. "Of course I'll help you. I feel sure Garland is innocent."

"You might be certain of that. As for me, I just work to get them off whether they're innocent or guilty. Makes no never mind."

Jeez, I hated that attitude. I know that everyone deserves a fair trial and all that, but I still hate to see the guilty ones get off scot-free just because of some oversight or mistake on the part of the police. As for me, I've got to believe in their innocence or I'm not wasting my time.

"So where do we go from here?"

"Come in to my office in the morning about nine and we'll talk about it."

I called Logan immediately.

As soon as I identified myself he said, "Let me guess. You want some time off."

"You're a mind reader, Logan. How did you know?"

"Because every time a friend of yours gets in trouble, you want to help them. Simple, my dear Watson."

"Well, I'm caught up at the office."

"And you never take a vacation so you have time coming to you."

He was right. I really couldn't afford to go on vacation, and I didn't have anyone to go with anyway.

"So you don't mind."

"It would be nice if your friends could give you prior notice they were going to be arrested so you could give me advance warning. But I guess that's not possible."

I knew he was kidding. To be truthful, he always got a kick out of being on the periphery of solving murder cases.

I WAS SITTING IN Bernard's office first thing the next morning. It was just down the hall from his wife Pamela's office where I'd been the spring before. She'd begged me to help when Bernard was arrested for the murder of my divorce lawyer, Evan McCandless. As you can imagine there was no love lost between the two men as Evan had urged me to take Bernard to the cleaners. But I'd been so mortified by the fact he'd dumped me that I didn't have the heart to fight it, and my settlement was just enough to pay for my condo and not much else. At least I knew I'd have a roof over my head even if I had to work till I was eighty-five to put food on the table and gas in the tank.

But in spite of the very real hurt and resentment I'd felt toward Bernard, I knew the man I'd lived with for thirty-three years couldn't be a murderer. And I had managed to prove that.

His office was quite a contrast to his wife's. Hers was an odd combination of feminine frills and sleek modern furniture. Her big, stainless steel and mahogany desk dominated the room, but the pale blue walls, yellow-flowered drapes and matching upholstered visitor's chair seemed utterly incongruous in that room. Watercolor paintings of tulips and daffodils were interspersed with diplomas. But at least it had some individuality.

Bernard's on the other hand was standard boring lawyer's office. Nothing but his degrees hung on the wall, and fat case files were stacked everywhere, on top of file drawers, in the corner of the room, at the edge of his desk, a homely piece that probably came from Office Depot. I wondered how he could find the file he wanted in this mess.

"Good morning," he said pleasantly as I took a seat. "Has Logan given you leave?"

Was this the dawn of a new relationship between us? Our conversations since the divorce had been pretty much like a fencing match, trading caustic remarks in a battle of one-upmanship.

"I had time coming. Can't afford to go on vacation, you know."

I could have bitten my tongue. If he was willing to call a truce, I should try to do likewise.

"Well, don't feel sorry for yourself. I can't find the time for dallying either."

He never took time off when we were married either. He was so caught up in his law practice, he thought himself indispensable. When I wanted a vacation, I joined a tour group on my own. I'm sure

Carruther, Mierjeski and Poag could manage for a few days without him, but he didn't believe it.

"So where do we go from here?" I asked.

"We need to look into Fulton Ridenhour's background. Garland told me about how you, his wife, and another board member from your association managed to stop his lawsuit cold. Not quite copacetic I understand."

"Hey, look, Joe Kernodle blindsided us. We knew nothing about what he planned to do."

"Well, that's old news now. Joe found out about his past. I'm more interested in the present. Talk to his neighbors. Find out if he had any friends."

"I'd be surprised if he did. He wasn't a very friendly guy."

"Find out who his enemies were, then."

"Did you know he embezzled money out in Missouri?"

"Garland told me about that. I've got a call in to the United Way in Kansas City to get the details."

"You know they never pressed charges then. Does he have any kind of an arrest record?"

"Not that I've been able to ascertain."

"Did he have any family?"

"He'd been divorced for several years. Had a daughter he was estranged from."

"Is she in the area? What about his ex-wife?"

"I'll let you find them. Talk to both of them and the neighbors."

"Okay, then. I guess I'll start with his neighbors since they're the closest."

I left Bernard's office which was downtown on South Greene Street and drove back home.

EIGHT

SINCE IT WAS TUESDAY morning I didn't know if I would find anyone at home on Fulton's street. I first went to the next door neighbor's. Since there was a For Sale sign in the front yard, I knew it had to belong to Bob what's-his-name who'd been unfortunate enough to leave out the pan of antifreeze. I knocked on the door a couple of times, but there was no answer. Curious, I looked around to see if anyone was watching me, but there wasn't another soul on the street. So I wriggled my way behind the nandina bushes and peered in the front window. The living room was empty. Bob had apparently moved out. Had he been so frightened of Fulton that he felt he needed to leave even though his house was still for sale? That would be an act of real desperation in this market. His house could sit empty for months, and that could have a devastating affect on his finances. Mack hadn't mentioned anything about him moving when I saw him at the reenactment on Sunday. So it must have just happened. I'd have to find out where Bob had gone and talk to him.

Lucky for me, Mack's wife was home. She answered

the door dressed in blue jeans and tee shirt. Both Thurstons were in their thirties; he was rather plain looking, but she was unusually attractive in spite of her casual attire. Her hair seemed to be naturally blond although it's next to impossible to tell the real thing anymore. But her fair skin and blue eyes were compatible with a Scandinavian heritage.

When I introduced myself and explained why I was there, she invited me in.

"I'm Vickie. I normally wouldn't be home but I'm taking a few days off," she explained as she led me toward a comfortable-looking chair. "I get more vacation than Mack does, so I take those extra days to get caught up around the house. What with two kids, a husband and a job, things can get quite out of control."

You could have fooled me. Her house appeared spotless. I live alone, and my house is never that neat. She must be one of those Supermoms they talk about.

"Can I offer you some coffee?" she asked. "I just made a pot."

Though I'd had a couple of cups before I left the house, I was ready for another so I told her yes.

While she was in the kitchen, I looked around the room. I thought of the HGTV shows I'd watched. This room could have stood up well to the ones on the decorating network with its dark red walls and white upholstered furniture. I would never have considered painting my walls such a strong color, but with touches of red accessories like pillows and glass bowls, it was striking. I wondered if she'd had a decorator or had done it herself. All these well decorated condos were giving me an inferiority complex.

I was bold enough to ask her when she returned with two cups of coffee and sugar and cream on a tray. She set it on a white hassock that served as a coffee table.

"I work for one of the furniture companies," she said. "I love it because I get discounts. Otherwise I couldn't afford this stuff," she said, waving her hand to indicate all the furnishings.

Nearby High Point is a center of the furniture industry, and huge furniture markets are held there every April and October for registered buyers. She probably was able to buy market samples which would save her hundreds of dollars. Even area stores open to the public often sell market samples although she could probably get even better discounts with her connection.

"I wanted to ask you about your next door neighbor. I know his name is Bob, but I don't know his last name," I said.

"Hayes. Poor Bob."

"It looks like he moved."

"Yesterday. Drove up in a rental truck with another guy first thing in the morning and started loading furniture. By mid-afternoon they were gone."

"Do you know where?"

"When I saw what was happening, I walked over. Asked him where he was going. He told me he'd rather not say. When I asked him if it had anything to do with Fulton's death, he almost freaked out. Apparently he didn't know Fulton had died. He'd been packing boxes all day Sunday and never watched the news."

"Do you know if anyone can verify he was home packing boxes?"

"Well, I assume his wife could. I didn't see her yesterday and figured she'd probably gone ahead to their new place to clean it up before they moved their furniture in."

"Why wouldn't he tell you where he was going?"

"At first it was because he didn't want Fulton to know where he was, he said. He was scared to death of him. Then when I told him Fulton was dead, he said he didn't want to get mixed up in the investigation so he'd just as soon not have the police know where he'd gone."

"Didn't he realize that makes him look suspicious?"

"He was so rattled, I don't think it occurred to him."

I wondered if it would be possible to track Bob down. He probably had a phone installed in his new place. Maybe Bernard could find out from the phone company. Then I realized how many people use only cell phones these days and don't even have a landline. Oh, my.

"Do you know where Bob works?" I asked.

"Yes, he works at Replacements Limited," Vickie said. "Second shift. That's why he was home during the day changing his antifreeze."

Surely I could find out from them where he now lived. Replacements is a large facility east of town on I-40 that sells replacements for china and silverware to people all over the world. The business, which was started in a private home, has grown to a multi-million dollar corporation, and they recently announced they would build a huge addition. The owner had found a niche and has since prospered hugely from it.

"And his wife. Does she work?"

"No. She suffers from multiple sclerosis. She has good days and she has bad ones. It's too unpredictable for her to work."

"What a shame. Is she fairly young?"

"They're both in their forties. No kids."

"So tell me what you know about Fulton. I understand he was a pretty obnoxious neighbor."

Vickie shook her head. "I suppose there's one in every neighborhood. But he was especially bad. Let his dog do his business in our yard every time he took him out for a walk."

"Mack had told me that. Thought he did it on purpose."

"I think he just liked to needle people."

"Who else did he needle?"

"In the summertime he'd sit out on his patio and turn his boom box volume up as high as it would go. Rap music. You can't tell me a guy his age was into rap music. He did it just to annoy everyone."

"Did people complain?"

"Lots of them did. It was brought before the homeowner's board last summer, and they threatened to evict him if it kept up. I don't know if they could have or not, but I guess he didn't want to test it. The music stopped."

"I can remember hearing some awful music over at my place and I live a couple of blocks away," I said. "I figured it was college students."

"And then he started parking so he straddled two parking spaces. They kept warning him not to do it, but he kept on. Finally, Rhonda got him towed. When he found out, he hit the roof."

"You don't want to mess with Rhonda," I said.

Vickie smiled. "You're so right."

"Well, the little contact I've had with her I could tell she was a piece of work. Do you know anything about Fulton's background? Did you know he'd been divorced and had an estranged daughter?"

"No, I wasn't friendly with him, so I never found out much about him. I don't think anyone around here did."

That reminded me of Joe's friend the PI who had looked into Fulton's background. I could talk to Joe and see if he uncovered anything about him besides the embezzlement.

"I really appreciate your help, Vickie," I said as I got up to leave.

"Now that we've met, come back again. I've always said we should have some kind of big neighborhood blowout like a cookout in the summer so we can all get better acquainted. Do you ever go to the cocktail hour at the clubhouse?"

"No, that's not really my thing."

"Mine either. We need get-togethers that don't include booze."

I wasn't opposed to responsible drinking, but I

stance ordered the duck confit salad, and I chose the herb gnocchi. We all had a glass of wine.

"Connie tells me you're working with Bernard," Garland said as he sipped his merlot.

"I am," I said, taking a sip of my sauvignon blanc.

"Isn't that a bit tricky working with your ex-husband?"

"A little, I have to admit. Though we kind of worked together, albeit unofficially, twice before." That wasn't really true because I did it behind his back the first time, and he was the suspect, not the lawyer, the second.

"But he's decided, finally, that I'm quite capable of helping him," I continued, "and since Constance really wanted me involved, I guess he felt he couldn't say no."

Garland looked concerned. "Your differences aren't going to get in the way, are they?"

I laughed. "No, they shouldn't. I'll have to admit I was mad as hell at him for a long time. But, you know, I can't go through life that way. It was only hurting me, not him. I've learned to suck it up and accept the situation. Bernard can be a pompous ass sometimes, but he is damn smart, and he would have risen to the top at the Public Defender's office if he'd stayed on."

"So why didn't he?"

"Bernard is not an idealist. He wanted the big bucks, and he couldn't get them in public service. He might not be the poster boy for noble-mindedness, but he likes to win cases, and he's very good at it. I think he'll do a good job for you."

Garland gave me a hopeful smile. "I trust your

judgment, Tommi. I guess if you're willing to work with him after what he did to you, then he must be good."

Evidently Constance had filled him in on all the gory details of my failed marriage.

The waiter brought our meals and we tucked into the food. My gnocchi was out of this world. The little square pastas were filled with herbs of some kind and mixed with fresh green peas, asparagus, mushrooms, and topped with goat cheese. I thought I'd died and gone to heaven. Constance and Garland seemed to be pleased with their meals as well.

"It seems criminal to bring up the subject while we're enjoying our food so much," Constance said, "but have you been able to find out anything yet? I know you just started."

"Criminal, huh? Was that a subconscious pun?" I was dragging my feet a bit, wondering if it was okay to share what I'd learned with them. But they were bound to find out about Bob moving, so I saw no harm in it.

She rolled her eyes. "Wasn't thinking."

"I give you Brownie points for being clever." It couldn't hurt to add a little levity to this serious situation. "Anyway, I talked to Mack Thurston's wife Vickie. Do you know her?"

"He brought her to the Christmas party the board gave. She seems very nice."

"Well, she told me Bob Hayes moved."

"Who's that?" Garland asked.

"He lived next door to Fulton. He's the one who left out the pan filled with antifreeze."

"Mack was at the reenactment on Sunday," Constance told Garland. "We saw him after you left to be in the battle. He told us about Bob, said he had his house up for sale because he was so scared of Fulton."

"He sold it that fast?" Garland asked. "That was lucky. No one else in our development can seem to unload theirs."

"Actually, no," I said. "He told Vickie he'd made plans last week to leave even though it hadn't sold, and he got a rental truck and carted all the stuff away yesterday."

"Yesterday!" he said, slapping the table. "That sounds damned suspicious."

"When Vickie asked him if he did it because of Fulton's death, he freaked out. Said he didn't know anything about it because he'd worked all day packing up stuff on Sunday and never heard the news."

"Likely story!" Constance's eyes were blazing. "I hope you're following up on that, Tommi!"

That was the danger of sharing information. I was afraid they were going to start telling me how to do my job. I'd be a little more circumspect the next time they asked me about the case.

"I will, of course. Only problem is he wouldn't tell her where he was going."

"Well, that sounds doubly suspicious. Don't you think the cops can find him?" Garland asked.

I didn't know how to say this, but I decided the only

way was straight out. "I believe they've settled on you as the suspect, Garland." I didn't say *perp,* because it sounds even worse although that's exactly what they thought he was. "I don't think they're looking in other directions."

Constance stared at him in anguish. "I can't believe it! I still can't believe it!"

I reached across the table and patted her hand. "I know it's going to come out all right," I said reassuringly, although I had no idea where this case was going.

To get their minds off of their troubles, I changed the subject. "You know I've heard their desserts are really good here."

Garland and Constance looked at each other. "We usually don't do sweets, but what the heck," Constance said. "Isn't chocolate supposed to release endorphins? I sure could use a bunch of those right now."

We asked for the dessert menu and we all ordered profiteroles, ice cream smothered in chocolate sauce. As delicious as it was, I'm not sure it enhanced my endorphin count when I looked at the sad faces across from me. And I doubted it was doing anything for them.

NINE

When we got back to the Merritts' house, Constance opened the car door the minute it stopped. "You know, I think I might have left the iron on. I'm so rattled these days. I'm going to run, but I do want to tell you how much I appreciate your help, Tommi."

"I'm flattered you want me, Constance. I'll do everything I can."

As she ran toward the house, I put my hand on Garland's arm. "Can I talk to you a minute?"

We were both still in the Prius, he in the driver's seat and I in the back. "Sure, Tommi. What's up?"

"It doesn't seem to me that the cops have enough to go on with the fact that your sword was used to kill Fulton. Particularly not after you told them about taking it off and laying it on the grass. Is there something you're not telling us?"

He'd turned to look at me and pinched his lower lip between thumb and forefinger in indecision. Finally he said, "You're right, Tommi. I didn't want Constance to know because she's worried enough as it is. I was so concerned about the two of you after your confrontation with Fulton over the lawsuit, I sent him an e-mail. I wasn't thinking very straight and my anger got the better of me. Of course I never expected that the police would confiscate my computer, find the e-mail, and consider it a possible prelude to murder."

"What on earth did you say?"

Garland looked embarrassed. "I hope you'll excuse the language. I don't generally talk like this around ladies. But my exact wording was, 'If you make any kind of threat against my wife again, I will cut off your nuts.' I guess when the cops heard Fulton had made threatening remarks the day of the reenactment, they thought I'd carried out my warning."

I'D LEARNED FROM GARLAND the name of Joe Kernodle's business. Guilford Printing Company was located off of West Market Street on Edwards Drive, a short street lined on both sides with brick buildings housing a variety of small businesses. The street rambles in an S curve between Market and Wendover.

I found Joe sprawled in an old-fashioned oak swivel chair when the girl at the front desk showed me into his office. With the chair tipped back, he had his feet propped on the edge of a battered oak desk cluttered with stacks of papers and assorted knick knacks mostly relating to UNC sports. The walls were covered with bulletin boards displaying various printed materials that his company produced. I could see a program for the reenactment among restaurant menus and flyers for art shows and flea markets. He didn't move but told me to have a seat in the equally ancient chair on the other side of the desk.

"So what brings you here?" He asked, holding a pencil chest high with both hands that he fingered like a flute, as if I had interrupted an important task. I doubted very much that he had been doing anything other than staring off into space before I came in.

"You've heard, I'm sure, about Fulton Riden-hour," I said.

"Looks like someone got totally fed up with him," he grinned as he spoke. So much for eulogizing the dead.

"I understand you do the printing for the reenact-ment of the battle. Do you attend it as well? I thought maybe you're a history buff."

"Hell, no. I spend my Sundays fishing. I've got a little boat I take out on Belews Lake."

"Does your wife go with you?" I had no idea whether he even had a wife, but I hoped to find out who was with him so I could verify his story.

"My wife left me two years ago. But that's okay. She hated to fish. Besides, I like to be alone. Good time to get away from the crowds."

Joe, a loner? Not quite what I'd pictured. So it could be a little tricky to check up on where he was on Sunday. I'd just have to take his word for it for now.

"I wanted to ask you what your PI friend found out about Fulton in addition to the fact he embezzled from the United Way."

Joe squinted at me. "What the hell for? The guy is dead."

"Garland's lawyer has asked me to help him get a little background information."

"Can't he check Fulton out himself?"

"Well, sure. But I thought it would also be helpful to find out what your friend learned. Every little bit helps you know."

Joe was really curious now. Was I making him nervous? "Why you?"

I didn't want to spell it out for him. He undoubtedly would sneer at my investigative background. I just said, "I have some experience in doing this, Joe. I've helped in a couple of other cases."

He put the pencil down, took his feet off the desk, and sat up. "You're a complicated lady, Tommi. You're full of surprises."

"Not really."

"I ought to charge you for the information. But since my friend gave it to me for free, I guess I can pass it along." I'm sure he wasn't kidding. I had a hunch he'd make a buck wherever he saw the opportunity.

"I'd appreciate it."

"For one thing he found out that Fulton had cheated on the bar exam when he took it in Missouri. There was a small fire at the place where it was given. Everyone was told to leave the exams on the table and evacuate the building and they would be notified where the exam would be continued the next day. Someone found out that Fulton had sneaked a copy out to look up the answers. He was barred from ever taking it there again. That's when he went to work for the United Way."

"I thought he took the bar several times and failed."

"He did. He took it twice after he moved to North Carolina and flunked it. He was taking it a third time, when somebody squealed on him and told the local bar what had happened in Missouri. So they threw him out."

"Do you know who it was who informed on him?"

"No. I had all I needed to get him off our case, so I told my guy he didn't have to bother to find out."

"Maybe Fulton knew and was threatening whoever it was."

"Entirely possible."

"Anything else? What about his ex-wife? And doesn't he have a daughter?"

"Yeah. The wife kicked him out about three years ago. She stayed married to the sorry son-of-a-gun for over twenty years. Don't know how she stood him for that long. That's when he moved to our neighborhood. She lives in Kirkwood, in the house they'd been in since they came to Greensboro."

Kirkwood is an older area off Lawndale Drive not too far from Cottage Place with modest but well-kept houses on deep lots. It's known as the neighborhood where the offspring of the wealthy buy starter homes to live in while they work their way up the ladder till they can afford to live in places like nearby Irving Park, the premiere enclave of the "powers-that-be."

"What's her first name? Did she keep her married name?"

"It's Donna Ridenhour. That's all I know."

"What about the daughter?"

"I guess the daughter had been in trouble for years. She dropped out of high school right after her parents split. She lives with some guy in a trailer east of town."

"And her name is?"

"Lana."

"Anything else you can tell me about Fulton?"

"Nah. Once I had the goods on him about the embezzlement, that's all I needed. Called my friend off the case. Might need him some other time, and he still owes me some favors."

In a way I was glad he had nothing else to tell me. His sleaziness was beginning to feel as if it were contagious. I thanked him and left.

There wasn't much more I could do since the day was getting on, and my fridge was completely bare. I stopped off at Fresh Market on my way home and picked up enough to get me through the next few days.

I WAS READING a Marcia Muller mystery when the phone rang around eight o'clock.

"Hi, Tommi. It's Frank."

His voice, as always, sent a little shiver up my spine. I hadn't talked to him in a couple of weeks as he'd been to Europe on business.

Frank was Bernard's first cousin, though I had never met him until a couple of years ago when his daughter,

Nina, had been arrested for the murder of her husband. The two men hadn't spoken in over thirty years because of a personal vendetta until Nina asked Bernard to represent her, and Frank came to town from Wisconsin to try and talk her out of it. The upshot of the whole sorry episode was that Frank and I worked together to find the evidence needed to absolve Nina although we had to do it behind Bernard's back. After that the two men had managed to come to a truce of sorts.

Then the next year, Bernard was accused of killing my divorce lawyer, Evan McCandless, during a disaster exercise at the Girl Scout camp. Again Frank came to help me find the real killer and almost lost his life in the bargain. That's when I realized how much the dear man meant to me. The only problem was that he lived hundreds of miles away and our relationship was maintained by e-mail and phone calls. Not the most satisfying of connections, but the best we could do under the circumstances.

"It's so good to hear your voice. How was the trip?"

"The trip was okay. But I have some bad news."

My heart did a little flip-flop in my chest. "What bad news, Frank? What's wrong?"

"Nina has been diagnosed with breast cancer."

I was stunned. Nina was only thirty-nine years old. "Why didn't she tell me?" Nina and I had become good friends in spite of our difference in ages. She lived in a huge mansion in Oak Ridge, a small town a few miles away, that her late husband, a very successful script-writer, had bought when they moved from California. Cap had loved ostentation, while Nina was a much more modest soul. But mansions weren't selling these days, and she hadn't been able to unload it so far. "We had lunch a couple of weeks ago. Did she know then?"

"She found out last week. But she wanted me to know first."

I could understand that as they were very close, especially since her mother had died of breast cancer a few years ago. Frank had taken a promotion offered him by American Communications System that sent him to Wisconsin. He needed to break away from the haunting memories of his wife's illness. That was before Nina and Cap moved back to North Carolina from California. Now his beloved daughter was facing the same diagnosis. It had to be devastating to them both.

"Oh, God, no. I'm just sick about that. How is she doing? What's the prognosis?"

"They won't know till after surgery of course. But since the lump is small, they feel she has a pretty good chance of beating it."

"She's a fighter, Frank. If I know her she has a good attitude."

"I'm coming down there, Tommi."

"I'm so glad. I know it will mean a lot to her. Do you have much vacation time coming?"

"I mean I'm moving back. ACS has found a job for me in Greensboro. I have to be there for her. She doesn't have anyone else." Nina and Cap had no children and her siblings were scattered far and wide.

I didn't know what to say. I was so torn between being thrilled that he was moving here and being devastated by the reason it was happening. Finally I said, "It's wonderful of you to do this for her. Where will you live?"

"For the time being I'll stay at her house. She's just rattling around in that huge place by herself, and I can be there to support her while she's recovering from surgery and going through treatment. When she's recovered," his voice broke a little, "which I know she's going to do, I'll find a place in Greensboro."

"When are you coming?"

"I'm flying in tomorrow. I have some vacation time coming to me, and Nina's surgery is scheduled for Friday."

"Let me pick you up."

"Nina's planning to. She wants to act as if everything is normal. I offered to take the shuttle but she wouldn't hear of it."

That sounded like the spunky Nina I knew. I didn't want to intrude on them. "Please let me know what I can do. If I know her, she won't want to impose on anyone, but I really want to help. And it would never be an imposition."

"Probably the best thing you can do is to cheer both of us up. I'll be in touch when I get there."

I didn't want to tell him about my investigation at

this point. He had enough on his mind as it was. Of course, when he got to town I'd have to explain.

Immediately after I hung up, I called Nina, but she didn't answer the phone. She was probably out playing bridge or going to a movie as if nothing was going wrong in her life.

TEN

WEDNESDAY MORNING dawned cold and blustery. Tee, who now slept on my bed, woke me up earlier than usual sniffing at my hair like it was a dead mouse. When he started licking it I was forced out of bed and into the shower. I wondered if there were remnants of shampoo that had attracted him. I can never understand why improbable objects like dirty socks or dead flowers turn him on. His tastes are eclectic to say the least.

I'd decided to try and locate Donna Ridenhour and talk to her. I also wanted to track down Bob Hayes, but it seemed the best bet was to go to Replacements after four when his shift began since no one knew where he'd moved.

So I did what any detective worth her salt would do: looked Donna up in the phone book. And sure enough she was listed on Liberty Drive. However, when I called her number, I got no answer. The next best thing I could think of was to canvass her neighbors and find out if she worked somewhere.

Liberty Drive is but a ten minute jaunt from my house. It runs off Lawndale Drive across from the spot which once housed the huge southeastern warehouse for Sears, but now is the home of another ubiquitous shopping area boasting a Target and Harris Teeter.

The nearby residents weren't thrilled when the stores went up, but since the old Big Bear Supermarket a few blocks away had long ago disappeared, it at least gave them a grocery store they could walk to. Since public transportation in Greensboro leaves a lot to be desired, a neighborhood grocery is a great asset.

I found her house not too far off Lawndale. It was a well kept modest single story ranch with white siding and green shutters. At the driveway entrance a group of azaleas were clustered which would be blooming in less than a month, and a Bradford pear was just beginning to show a little white, usually the first harbinger of all the glorious flowering trees and shrubs that turn Greensboro into a gardener's paradise in April. If I could just get through the rest of March, a month of notoriously unpredictable weather, I'd be into my favorite time of the year.

I parked in the drive and went up on the front stoop to ring the bell, just in case Donna had been busy elsewhere in the house when I phoned. But no one answered the door. I crossed the yard to the next-door neighbor's, another small ranch painted pale blue. This time an elfin-faced child of about three opened the door. She looked up at me, smiled, and said, "Hi." I wondered if it was safe to let little ones answer the door in this time of child abductions and what-have-you. Then I had to consider that I was overreacting because of the nature of the work I had been doing tracking down murderers.

At any rate, her mother was right behind her with a baby in her arms. The little one just ran faster than her mother could. The young woman was dressed in chinos and a striped shirt, her black hair pulled back in a ponytail. The baby looked to be about six months old, and I couldn't tell if it was a boy or a girl.

"May I help you?" she said with a smile. I guess I look benign enough to have reassured her I wasn't up to mischief.

"I'm trying to find Donna Ridenhour," I said. "No one's at home. Do you know if she works?"

"Yes, she does. She's a saleslady at Coldwater Creek in the Shops at Friendly."

"Did you know her ex-husband?"

Her smile vanished and a frown creased her forehead. She said nothing, but just nodded grimly.

"Could I ask you a few questions about him?"

She looked doubtful, but the baby was starting to squirm and I knew she wanted to close the door against the chill wind. "May I ask who you are and why you want to know?"

"If I could just step in a minute before you all freeze to death."

She hesitated, but stepped back. "Sure, I guess so." She put her free arm on the little girl's shoulder to steer her back into the room. "Come on, Steph, let the lady come in."

The living room was furnished in what appeared to be hand-me-down furniture, but quality pieces. I had a hunch this family was one of the future movers and shakers in the community. She had that indefinable quality about her that spoke of a privileged upbringing.

"My name is Tommi Poag," I said. "I live on Cottage Place, off of Lake Jeannette Road. I'm helping the lawyer who's defending the husband of a friend of mine."

She extended her hand to shake mine. "I'm Gretchen Saunders," she said. "Won't you have a seat? Let me put the baby in his crib. He's due for a nap."

I recognized the name. I was pretty sure her father-in-law was one of the businessmen who ran with the inner circle of Greensboro's elite. I sat down on the beige couch and gazed around the room. The little girl had followed her mother down the hall to the nursery. Except for a small pile of toys in front of a television set, the room was neat and clean. I wondered if she could afford maid service or if the parents provided it. I figured she had her hands full with two small children.

Gretchen was back in a couple of minutes with Steph trailing behind. "Can I offer you a drink?" she asked. "I have some fresh coffee already made."

I had become a little chilled in the raw March wind, so I accepted her offer. "I take it black."

She disappeared into the kitchen. This time the

child stayed behind, looking at me with curious eyes. "Are you my mommy's friend?" she asked.

"I don't know your mommy, but I hope we can become friends. What's your brother's name?"

"Boo."

"That's nice," I said. Visions of *To Kill a Mockingbird* floated through my mind.

Gretchen returned with two cups, handing one to me. "His name is Borden. But she likes to call him Boo. Now what can I do for you?"

"I'm trying to find out as much as I can about Fulton Ridenhour. The lawyer I work for represents the man accused of killing him. That man happens to be a friend of mine, and I have every reason to believe he's innocent."

"What makes the police think he did it then?"

"Circumstantial evidence. Someone set him up."

"Oh, dear. That's terrible."

"So you knew Fulton?"

"Unfortunately, yes."

"And what can you tell me about him?"

"He and Donna and their daughter were living next door when we moved here eight years ago. They used to fight a lot, and in the warm weather when the windows were open you could hear them shouting. Actually Donna is a pretty nice person, but she has a temper and when Fulton started yelling at her, she'd yell right back. I knew he took the bar exam a couple of times and flunked it, and I think his frustration level was so high that he took it out on her and his daughter."

"Took it out? You mean physical abuse?"

"I think he slapped her around some. A lot of emotional abuse too. I mean how long can you put up with someone who blames you for everything?"

"I understand they were married for about twenty years."

Gretchen shook her head as if unable to understand why that had happened. "I think Donna was afraid she couldn't support herself and Lana if she left him."

The same sad story that happens to so many women. The one who holds the purse strings has the upper hand.

"What finally made her kick him out then?"

"When the local bar association barred him from taking the exam again. They found out that he'd tried to cheat on one when he lived in Missouri. Evidently Donna didn't know about that. I guess it was the final straw."

Steph had sidled up to me to hand me a doll. It looked as though it had been well loved. I took it from her, smoothed down the matted hair, and said, "What a nice doll. And what's her name?"

"Sugar."

"Sugar? That's an unusual name."

"It's 'cause she's so sweet."

"Go on and play now, Steph, so Mommy and the lady can talk," Gretchen told her.

She obediently took the doll from my hands and sat

back down on the floor to cuddle her. Once in a while even to this day, when I see a child as sweet as Steph it brings up the old yearning I have for the children I was unable to conceive. I did my best to banish the thought from my mind.

"What about Fulton's daughter?" I asked.

"Lana dropped out of school right after her parents split. She worked as a waitress at IHOP until she met some guy and moved in with him."

"Do you know where she lives?"

"Donna told me east of Greensboro somewhere. That's all I know."

"Anything else you can think of?"

"Just that Fulton worked at Home Depot and he was always bringing stuff home like boxes of tiles, lighting fixtures, bathroom towel bars and such. It might have been on the up and up, but I sometimes wondered if he was stealing stuff from them."

"Do you think anyone else in the neighborhood could add to what you've told me?"

"I doubt it. He's been gone over three years, and until the recent slowdown in home sales, a lot of the houses changed hands. I can't think of anyone who knew him."

I thanked her, patted Steph on the head, and left.

I DROVE STRAIGHT TO the Shops at Friendly located on Friendly Avenue, a tribute to the many Quakers who live in our area. Coldwater Creek is one of my favorite stores, and I hoped I could resist the temptation to buy something while I was there. I usually cannot.

The Shops at Friendly was a recent addition to Friendly Center, a large outdoor shopping center that has existed for over fifty years. When Burlington Industries, whose headquarters was adjacent to the shopping center, went belly up, its award-winning building, a huge pink glass box framed with crisscrossed external steel girders, was imploded and its beautifully landscaped lawns supplanted by fashionable mid-price-range stores and restaurants. Preservationists were not happy with the loss of another landmark building, but that's what passes for progress.

I took Green Valley Road, passing the Proximity Hotel where we'd had lunch the day before, to the shopping center. Luckily I found a parking place near Coldwater Creek, not always an easy accomplishment. I asked the first clerk that I met to point out Donna Ridenhour to me. She was helping another customer, so I browsed through the sale rack, a dangerous thing to do. I have little self control when it comes to sales in my favorite stores. But before I got carried away with "finds," the customer left and I went over and introduced myself.

Donna was a few years younger than I am, but a difficult life had left its marks on her face. Unhappiness had made a permanent scowl line between her brows even when she smiled at me. Her hair was salt-and-pepper drab cut in a short bob and held back by a headband. I noticed that her hands shook slightly as she clasped them together in an attempt, I supposed, to still them.

"I wondered if I could take you to lunch," I said. It was getting close to noon.

She looked startled. "Well, that's nice of you, but…whatever for?"

I kept my tone low so no one else could hear. "I've been asked by the lawyer who represents the man arrested for killing your ex-husband to look into Fulton's background."

She looked wary. "The police have talked to me already."

"I'm sure they have. And eventually we might learn what they found out through the D.A.'s office. But we also need to do our own investigation." I loved saying "we." It sounded so official, something my investigations have never been before.

She sighed. "I get off at one o'clock. I guess I could meet you. Where do you want to go?"

"How about Mimi's? But I'll pick you up here." The restaurant was just a block away. And it had deep booths where we could talk privately. I was glad she said one o'clock because the crowds should be thinning out by then.

"Okay."

With a little over an hour until we could meet, the temptation was just too great. I found a pair of pants, a cute red knit top, and a great quilted jacket on sale. I reasoned that Bernard was going to pay me some-

thing for my work, and therefore I shouldn't feel
guilty. I was so eager to help the Merritts, I'd never
asked him how much. But in the past I'd investigated
murders for nothing. So I was ahead of the game even
if it was merely a pittance.

We found a booth out of hearing of other diners. I
ordered the Asian choppèd salad and Donna had the
Blue Cheese and Walnut one. The dangerous thing
about Mimi's Café is the fact they serve huge delicious
muffins along with the salad. I asked for a carry-out
box immediately, hoping that by putting it out of sight
I wouldn't be as likely to eat it there and could save it
for breakfast—perhaps two or three breakfasts.

We chatted about clothes and the weather and other
safe topics while we waited for our food. She seemed
like a nice but troubled woman. I guess anyone would
have been troubled who'd lived with Fulton for twenty
years.

When we were served I said, "I know this must be
a sensitive subject for you, but I'm trying to find out
as much as I can about your former husband. Maybe
that will lead me in the direction of the person who
killed him."

"So you don't think it's the one they arrested?"

"I know him. He's a teacher and a very nice guy.
It's inconceivable to me that he could have done it. I'm
helping his lawyer find information to exonerate him."

"Oh, my. That does make a difference, doesn't it?
I'd hate to have the wrong man be punished for it.
Fulton caused enough pain in his lifetime. I'd hate to

have his death hurt some innocent person too. I was a fool to stay married to him for so long, but when you have a child, somehow it just seems too difficult to leave. Particularly when you have little money. But that was a huge mistake."

"A huge mistake how?"

"Lana, my daughter, has paid the price. I don't think Fulton ever sexually abused her, at least she never told me so, but he certainly abused her emotionally, the same as he did me. She held up under it pretty well for a long while, otherwise I would have left him sooner, but when she got to high school she just kind of fell apart. Dropped out and got hooked up with a guy I don't think is a good influence. She lives with him in a trailer out toward Gibsonville and I rarely see her."

"Where do they work?"

"He repairs motorcycles at a dealership. Lana says she can't find a job. I don't know how hard she's tried. But she doesn't have much in the way of job skills." Donna looked ineffably sad.

"Do you think I could talk to her? About her dad?"

Donna looked out the window for a while with a faraway stare. Then she shrugged her shoulders. "I'm not crazy about the idea. She's trying very hard to get over him. But I wouldn't want an innocent man go to jail. If you feel that it would help you, I could give you her address."

"I'd appreciate that," I said. I was a little surprised she would do that, but I guess I'd successfully appealed to her sense of fairness. Garland could use all the fair shakes he could get.

She opened her purse, pulled out a tiny notebook and tore out a page. She scribbled an address on it and handed it to me.

"Thanks, Donna. I have a few more questions if you don't mind. They shouldn't be quite so personal."

She gave me a weak smile. "It's always hard to air your dirty linen to others. At least it's hard for me. I was never one to give my friends blow-by-blow descriptions of my family life. I always thought it was nobody else's business."

"I agree with you under most circumstances, except when it comes to murder. Unfortunately, sometimes even when you're an innocent bystander, you have to tell the sordid details in court if you're forced to. Let's hope we can figure this one out before it comes to that." I hoped that was enough of an incentive to make her more comfortable talking to me. I reached over and patted her hand as added reassurance.

She seemed to relax a little. We'd finished our salads. "How about some dessert?" I asked.

"Mmmm, I know I shouldn't, but I think I will," she said. I was heartened by that. At least she wasn't anxious to leave and conclude our conversation.

We both ordered Mimi's S'mores. I excused myself on the grounds it would show solidarity with Donna, though my inner conscience was having a fit.

"Let me ask you something about Fulton that's

puzzled me. Why on earth was he interested in participating in the reenactment? Somehow that seems out of character for him."

She shook her head, a grimace on her face. "That puzzled me too. He started doing that just before we split. But I should have known why. It was another one of his scams. I found out that the material he was selling wasn't what he said it was."

"I was told it was pure wool that had to be imported from Holland because you can't get it around here."

"Well, it wasn't. It was a much cheaper mix of wool and other fibers that cost him far less than he said. He didn't make big bucks from it. But Fulton was willing to cheat people for the joy of putting one over on them. And I think it played to his ego to dress up in eighteenth century clothes and be a part of something like that."

"Tell me about his dog. The one that died."

"His dog died? I didn't know that." She seemed very surprised.

I told her about being on the board of the condo association and about the lawsuit he brought when Sir Martingale got into antifreeze.

"Oh, my gosh. Poor little Marty." She choked up and a single tear ran down her cheek. She wiped it away with her napkin.

"Marty?"

"That was short for Sir Martingale."

"So you did know the dog."

"Yes, it's hard to believe, but Fulton's mom Rebecca was a nice gal. We always got along well, and we kept up our relationship after Fulton and I split. So I'd see the dog when I visited her."

"You knew then that she'd asked Fulton to take the dog if she died. Had she been ill? Was her death expected?"

"She'd had a couple of heart attacks. With her diabetes, she was kind of treading on thin ice. Her health was really poor."

"So that's why she'd made arrangements for your ex to have the dog."

"Actually no. She wanted me to have him. But there was nothing in her will or anything to indicate she'd told me that. When I went to claim him, Fulton told me it was his by right of inheritance. I knew he didn't like dogs much, and I thought he did it just to spite me."

"I'm sure he took Marty because he thought he could make some money off of him as a stud," I said. "That seems typical of him."

"Well, it couldn't have been out of the goodness of his heart. You know, it wouldn't surprise me if he somehow arranged for that so-called accident to happen. He probably had him insured for a lot. That way he could make money off him without having to take care of him."

"I sincerely doubt that. He'd have to be in collusion with his neighbor, and from all accounts the neighbor was not only devastated by it but scared that Fulton might retaliate." The fact that Bob Hayes had moved out without having sold his house was testimony to his fear.

Donna played with her straw as she pondered that idea. "It was probably a bonus that Marty drank the antifreeze. He no doubt just meant for the dog to run away."

"What makes you think that?"

"Because he always kept him in a dog cage when he was gone. Fulton must have known when the painters were coming and left Marty out of the cage knowing he'd slip out the door the minute he had the chance. Marty would try to go back to Rebecca's house where he was loved."

"How do you know about the dog cage?"

"Lana told me. She went over to her dad's a couple of times to ask him for some money and saw him there. She thought it was cruel to keep him in the cage so much."

Her theory made a lot of sense. But it only reconfirmed what a despicable guy Fulton was. I couldn't see how it would help to solve his murder.

ELEVEN

I TOOK HER BACK TO Coldwater Creek and dropped her off. It was too early to drive to Replacements since Bob's shift didn't start until four o'clock, so rather than go home I went to Bicentennial Garden to think things over. Located only a few blocks away on Hobbs Road, it's one of the loveliest parks in Greensboro with its meandering paths, a small wedding pavilion, and its scent garden among many beautiful flower beds. It was too early for much bloom but colorful pansies brightened the walkways as they did in yards and public places all over Greensboro during the winter months.

I sat on a bench to watch the birds and squirrels hop and run about with their bird and squirrel duties while I mentally went over my conversations with those close to Fulton. Most of all I'd learned that Fulton was even more despicable than I had first realized. In addition to his frivolous lawsuit against our condo board when he'd probably set up the scenario for his dog to get loose, he'd tried to con his way through life from stealing a bar exam to cheating his fellow reenactors to possibly stealing from his employer. He also treated his wife and daughter cruelly. I couldn't quite imagine that Donna could have killed her husband. She might have wanted to at one time or another, but it would have happened before now. She was rebuilding her life without him, and apparently had not had any contact with him for some time. I'd reserve my opinion about their daughter until I'd had a chance to meet her.

The reenactors were, as far as I knew, oblivious to the fact the material he was selling them wasn't the pure wool he claimed it to be; but even if they knew, it would hardly lead to his murder.

And if anyone found out he'd been stealing items at work, they'd have canned him, not killed him.

At this point the only motive for murder that I could think of was for one that had not been committed: Fulton might have wanted to kill Joe not only for denying him the opportunity to sue the board, but because he humiliated him and could use the knowledge of his embezzlement against him at any time. Had Fulton threatened Joe and Joe killed him out of fear? That was something that had to be explored.

I tried to reach Nina but I got no answer again. She might have been at the airport to meet Frank's plane. Since I would be interviewing Bob Hayes soon and my phone would be turned off, I didn't leave a message. I hoped I could reach them in the evening for I was terribly concerned about her and anxious to see Frank again.

I finally left the peaceful garden and drove toward Replacements on I-40, stopping for gas on the way. I had to remember to collect receipts to present to Bernard. With the cost of gas these days, I was glad to be able to include them as a business expense. What a high it was to earn some money for doing what I'd done before for free only because I was determined to see an innocent person exonerated.

It was a little after four when I pulled into the company's parking lot. Inside I found myself in a huge room where tables and shelves glittered with crystal and silver and dinnerware so colorful the space looked like a garden in bloom.

The company which began twenty-seven years ago at founder Bob Page's home now has an inventory of over twelve million items from which customers can replace broken or missing pieces or add to their collections. Known for its employee-friendly atmosphere, Replacements allows workers to bring their dogs to work. I imagine it would be quite a disaster if they allowed cats. I could see Tee crashing through displays of expensive china, though I'll have to admit he's never broken anything at home. But with a building the size of seven football fields full of breakables it would be tempting fate.

I asked the woman at the information desk if I could speak with Bob Hayes.

"May I ask why you wish to do so? He's not out on the sales floor, but in back."

"It's an urgent personal matter," I said.

She picked up a phone, dialed a number and spoke for a moment in a low tone.

"He'll be right out," she said with a smile.

Within five minutes, a fortyish slightly pudgy man came rushing up to the desk, and the receptionist pointed toward me.

"Is something wrong?" he asked, obviously upset. "Margot said it was something important of a personal nature." His baby face was glowing pink from either from concern or exertion—or both.

I hadn't thought about how alarming that must have sounded. "No, no," I said. "There's no emergency or anything. I just need to talk to you in private, and I didn't know how else to find you."

Relief flooded his features. "Thank goodness," he said. "I guess I overreacted, but I'll explain that to you back in my office." He flicked his eyes toward Margo signaling he didn't want her to overhear our conversation.

I let him lead me to the back of the enormous building which was a beehive of activity. He took me into a small office and closed the door, pulling out a wooden chair in the corner for me to sit. He plopped down behind a desk and wiped perspiration from his face with a handkerchief. Lying in a doggie bed in the opposite corner was a tiny Yorkie.

"Sorry," he said. "I'm not usually so nervous, but I've recently been in a situation that has me rather upset."

"Fulton Ridenhour," I said.

His blue eyes opened wide. He'd have been a nice looking man if he'd lost about forty pounds. At the rate he was sweating, I thought he could possibly do just that. "You know about him?"

"I live a couple of blocks from where your condo was, and I'm on the association board," I said. "By the way, my name is Tommi Poag."

He took a minute to try and place me. "I don't recall hearing your name."

"I'm brand new on the board. Just in time to go through the fiasco with Fulton."

He wiped at his face again with the now-soaked handkerchief. "That man terrified me. I never liked him, but when his dog died, I was fearful for my life to say nothing of Baby's." He gestured toward the little dog that looked up at the mention of her name and seemed to smile.

I didn't want to tell him at this point that it was possible Fulton arranged for his dog to escape, that he had intended to sue because Sir Martingale ran away. The antifreeze was a freaky twist to his plot. But apparently Fulton had embraced the coincidence.

"Is that why you moved so abruptly?" I asked.

"Yes, I was scared. And my wife was even more so. She has a medical condition, and being under stress just makes it worse. And Baby here managed to scoot out the door now and then if we weren't real careful. I knew he would do something dreadful to her if he could."

I remembered I'd been told his wife had MS.

"But you actually moved *after* Fulton was killed," I said.

"That's true. But I didn't know about it till the next morning when I was loading the truck. A neighbor told me."

"I know. I talked to Vickie Thurston. She says you were dead set on getting out of there, even though your place hadn't sold."

"We'd already rented the new place and my wife was there getting it ready. The furniture was almost loaded. Why would I want to stay?"

"It's just that it sounded like you were avoiding talking to the police."

"Not true."

"Vickie told me you didn't want to get caught up in the investigation. Were you afraid they might have thought you had a motive?"

He grimaced. "Maybe I did say something to the effect I didn't want to get involved. That was mostly for my wife's sake. She's my primary concern. If they had wanted to talk to me, they could have found me here the same as you did. Besides, I heard they arrested someone else."

"That's why I'm talking to you, Bob. I'm working with his lawyer. We're sure the police have the wrong man."

Bob looked anxious again. "Well, I hope you don't think I had anything to do with it."

"I don't," I said, though I wasn't ruling anyone out at this time. "I just wondered if you could tell me anything about Fulton that could help me."

He tugged at his earlobe as though it might prime

the pump for some ideas. "I obviously wasn't close to the guy. He always went around with kind of a swagger, the way bullies do when they want to prove they're the toughest guys around."

"Did you see anything more specific? Any kind of suspicious behavior?"

Now he folded the damp handkerchief into smaller and smaller squares on the desk top. Bob seemed to need to keep his hands busy to help him think. "I sometimes saw him unload boxes into his house at night. He and I worked the same shift and so I'd occasionally come home at the same time Fulton did. I always wondered if he paid for whatever was in those boxes."

Since two people had now told me that, it seemed more likely to be true.

"Anything else?"

"A number of times there would be a car parked in front of his place when I got home from work about one in the morning, and twice I saw someone get out and hurry into the house."

Aha! That sounded promising.

"Do you know who it was?"

"No. It was too dark to tell. But they seemed so furtive about it. After all, he's single. So it made me wonder why the secrecy."

"Did you ever see the car there during the day?"

"No. It was a Ford I think, not even sure of the model or year. It looked black but could have been dark blue I guess."

"You never got a look at the license plate, I suppose." Since he wasn't even sure about the model I had little hope he would have noticed that.

"Didn't pay attention. It wasn't like they were doing anything illegal. But I just thought it was kind of strange."

"Would you mind if I talk to your wife, Bob? She might have seen things that you didn't."

He seemed to agonize over the decision.

"Go easy on her, will you, if I tell you how to reach her?"

Did he think I had browbeat him? I thought I'd been the essence of cool. "Of course I will."

He wrote an address and telephone number on a memo pad, tore it off and handed it to me.

I HIT RUSH-HOUR TRAFFIC trying to get back into Greensboro which had me anxious to get home and find out if Frank had gotten to town yet. I'd checked my cell phone for messages as soon as I got in my car, but there was nothing. If he'd tried to call me at work, Logan would have told him I had taken some time off, and Frank might have thought it was in order to be with them. I wished it were true because now that I was working for Bernard, I wouldn't be able to spend as much time with Nina and Frank that I would like.

There was nothing on my home phone either, so I tossed one of my frozen dinners into the microwave and listened impatiently to the news. There was nothing about Fulton's murder.

Apparently it was off the radar for a while now that Garland had been arrested.

It was 7:30 when Frank called. "Nina and I are on our way out of the airport. Would it be all right to come by your place?"

All right? Was he kidding? "I can't wait to see you both."

They were there in twenty minutes. I hugged them both, trying to keep back tears of both concern and joy. I felt so conflicted about the situation; why did it have to be Nina's health scare that brought Frank back to town?

Nina looked wonderful as always. Tiny and slender with large green eyes, she still looked more like seventeen than thirty-eight. Her pale blond hair was pulled back in a pony tail that somehow looked elegant on her, and dressed in a pair of pale green slacks and beige cashmere sweater she looked as if she'd stepped from the pages of a fashion magazine.

Frank is not as striking as his daughter, but he's definitely above average in looks. About five foot ten with salt-and-pepper hair that comes to a gentle widow's peak, the only trait he shares with his cousin Bernard, he has the most infectious smile with a sweet disposition to go with it. Frank is no matinee idol but probably the most decent and caring man I've ever known. And his pleasant features reflect his good-natured personality.

When they were settled on my sofa, I picked up Tee

and sat in my bentwood rocker. I'd offered them refreshments which they'd turned down.

It's hard to know what to say to someone who's facing a frightening medical emergency. You're always unsure whether she wants to discuss it or not. So I decided to ask that question directly. "Do you want to talk about it Nina? I'll certainly understand if you don't."

She smiled, which floored me. But I shouldn't have been surprised. One of the things I've always loved about Nina is her way of being candid. "Of course I'll talk about it. I wouldn't want to bore most people with my problems, but I've always been able to unload on you."

"Well, it goes both ways. I've been known to dump on you as well."

"So you have. But that's what brought us together in the first place."

That was true. Soon after I met her we had lunch together on the first anniversary of my divorce. My hurt and shame came spilling out of me unexpectedly that day, which turned out to be a cathartic experience. She, in turn, shared with me tales of her late husband's indiscretions. We had a good group cry.

Frank sat quietly by, letting the conversation unfold between the two of us.

"So when did you find out about this cancer?" I asked.

"I felt a lump a couple of weeks ago so they did a biopsy. I guess I've been vigilant ever since Mom's cancer."

"The surgery is on Friday?"

"At Moses Cone outpatient surgery center."

"Outpatient? You've got to be kidding."

"That's why I'm here," Frank said. "The insurance companies won't pay for an overnight stay."

"There's a petition being sent around through e-mail trying to get Congress to do something about that," Nina said. "Only it's too late to help me."

"Well, that sucks big time," I said. I wondered if the people who set the guidelines for medical insurance ever had to go through this experience themselves. Surely if they did, they would have a little more compassion.

"Do you know yet whether it will be a lumpectomy or mastectomy?" I would not ordinarily ask this question, but with our difference in ages I felt as much a mother figure to Nina as I did a good friend.

"It'll depend on what they find. But either way I'll have radiation and possibly chemo. But enough about me. What's happening with you, Tommi?"

Nina seemed eager to change the subject, and I thought a blow-by-blow description of the past few weeks would serve to take her mind off her troubles. So I told them the story of Fulton Ridenhour with all the embellishments from the beginning when I first got on the homeowners' board.

"You mean Bernard actually asked you to work for him?" Frank sounded incredulous.

"Grumpy old Bernard?" Nina added.

"As impossible as it seems, he did," I said. "But, of course, Garland is a friend of mine, so I'm very anxious to clear his name. And his wife specifically asked Bernard to let me help."

Nina chuckled. "That never meant much in the past."

"People do mellow. Even Bernard," I said.

"I suppose," agreed Nina, "though it seems highly unlikely."

Frank was looking solemn now. "I don't know, Tommi. You've had some narrow escapes when you've done this before. Are you sure it's wise?"

Of course he wouldn't say so, but Frank had suffered far more than I did when he tried to help me. He'd been hit by a car that was aiming for me and was in a coma for a few days. I was touched by his concern. "You know I'll be careful, Frank. Honestly, the scariest person connected to this case so far is the guy who was killed."

"That's when it becomes dangerous. It's the people you're not afraid of who could harm you because your guard is down."

"I'll watch my back," I said.

"Let me work with you when Nina doesn't need me," Frank said. "She's going to be tied up tomorrow with some pre-surgery tests, and she's already told me she wants to drive herself to the hospital for them."

"Are you sure, Nina?" I asked her.

"There's no point in Dad having to sit around in the waiting room for me. I'm perfectly capable of going by myself," she said. "I think it's a great idea for him to be with you." Knowing Nina, she wanted to distract Frank from his worry over her.

"It's settled then," Frank said. "Now we need to go get a bite to eat. You might as well starve as far as the airlines are concerned. Do you want to join us?"

I knew they needed some time alone. "I just had a mouth-watering gourmet frozen meal. All filled up. Thanks anyway."

"Yeah, sure." Nina laughed. "Mouth watering and gourmet? I think not."

"It keeps me going," I said.

"That's how she keeps her trim figure," Frank said with a wink. "I'll give you a call in the morning."

After they left, I called the Merritts to catch them up on the day's interviews. I felt that I needed to keep them in the loop as much as possible.

I WAS READING THE PAPER and having my normal breakfast: Honey Bunches of Oats with bananas, juice, and coffee when Frank called.

"Hi," he said. "What's the drill for today?"

"There are two people I'd like to talk to," I said. "Fulton's estranged daughter is one. She lives with a boyfriend over near Gibsonville. Bob Hayes's wife is the other. They were Fulton's next-door neighbors who moved out the day after the murder. I talked to Bob yesterday. Since he works the second shift, he'd be home now. I'd rather talk to his wife alone."

"So let's go to Gibsonville."

"Sounds like a plan."

"I'll be there at ten."

I decided I had time to do at least one load of laundry before Frank came. I have a way of waiting until my wardrobe, limited as it is, is almost depleted before I think of doing a wash. Since housekeeping is one of the least interesting occupations in the world, I generally forget to do those things that keep it going.

I was stuffing a load of dark clothing into my stack unit when the phone rang.

It turned out to be Rhonda. I hadn't talked to her since Constance, Joe and I had met with Fulton over the lawsuit. Our next board meeting wasn't scheduled until next week.

"I have a favor to ask of you," she began.

Oh, no. I didn't feel like doing Rhonda a "favor." The last one, meeting with Fulton, had turned out to be a fiasco.

"I don't know, Rhonda," I said.

"Let me explain before you turn me down," she said in her officious way. "Fulton never changed his will after his divorce, so everything goes to his ex-wife Donna. I just talked to her, and she said that although she plans to sell the condo and welcomes whatever money she'll get out of that, she has no interest whatever in his belongings. It would bring back too many bad memories to go through all his stuff. She said she'd give me the key and we could do whatever we want with his furniture and so on."

I was glad that Donna was going to get something for having put up with the SOB for so many years.

And I could understand why she didn't want to deal with his personal effects. But I wondered what this had to do with me.

"Okay," I said.

"Well, I figured we could have a yard sale and make a little money for the homeowners' association. He's bound to have had a few things worth something, and we always can use some extra bucks. Would you be willing to help with that?"

Jeez. That really sounded like fun. "Why are you asking me, Rhonda?"

I should not have said that. Since I agreed to be on the board, I should accept whatever assignment was given to me. But this one sounded like a bummer. From what I saw, most of his furniture looked pretty junky.

"All the others already have multiple assignments or are heads of committees. And I thought since you're new, this might give you a chance to get to know the other members better. Once you've looked over his things, you can get a few of them to help you plan a sale."

"How soon do I have to do this?"

"No rush on the sale, but I'd like to have some idea of what he's got as soon as possible so we can begin to make plans. I'll be getting the key from Donna today so you can go see what's in his place. I'd like you to make some kind of inventory. That will give us an idea of what's worth selling and what might go to Goodwill. Though I've learned from experience, people will buy almost anything at a yard sale even if you think it should go to the dump."

It suddenly occurred to me that getting access to Fulton's home might be a very good thing. The police had probably gone through it, but with a suspect on hand so early in the investigation, they might not have been very thorough. No telling what I might find.

"Okay, Rhonda. I guess I could handle it. When could I get the key?"

"I'll bring it to you this evening."

I wondered if Fulton had left any secrets in his home.

TWELVE

FRANK SHOWED UP in a rental white Toyota Camry.

"So when are you going to bring your own car down here?" I asked him as we headed down Lawndale and Battleground toward Wendover Avenue. He insisted on driving.

"No point in putting miles on your car," he'd said. "I decided to leave it in Wisconsin till I'm ready to buy a house down here. And that depends on how Nina gets along with her surgery. It could be pretty soon or it might be a while. I don't want to get into the move as long as she needs me to stay with her."

We talked about things in general as we headed east on Wendover which turns into Route 70 going toward Gibsonville, a typical small North Carolina town. I occasionally go there to the Deloache factory outlet, a warehouse open to the public a few days a month featuring clothing, especially dressy women's jackets, at rock bottom prices. Although most of the textile mills are long gone from our area, numerous outlets are still around. And I'm an inveterate bargain hunter.

We followed the road that had been the main route to Burlington before the interstate system was built.

I-40 now serves as the main artery between the two cities. Route 70, or Burlington Road as it is known, has languished as a two lane highway for many years bordered by intervals of businesses and farmland. Twenty-five minutes of driving got us to the turn-off to Gibsonville, and we drove through the little town to Route 61 which heads north. Lana Ridenhour lived on 61 with her boyfriend.

A short way out of town we passed a vineyard on the right with a sign welcoming visitors to take a tour. This is the new face of North Carolina. Though it was once covered with tobacco farms in this area, many farmers have given up the crop which is no longer as lucrative and turned to growing grapes. Sixty-some vineyards dot the landscape, especially in the western and central regions of the state with a few in the southeast, and the wineries and their tasting rooms are popular destinations for locals and tourists alike.

I watched for house numbers on the mailboxes as Frank drove as slowly as he dared down the highway. Only two or three motorists honked at us in disgust and darted in front of us as soon as they could see far enough ahead to pass. One barely averted a head-on collision as he swerved back into our lane in front of our car. That's why I hate to look for unfamiliar addresses.

"The next driveway should be it," I said, pointing to a dirt path that led off into the trees on our right.

The driveway was heavily rutted, and I gave silent thanks we weren't driving my car. It would surely need a front end alignment had it gone down this path. A rusty single wide trailer was hidden behind the first row of trees. Wooden steps, grey from years of exposure to the weather, looked barely substantial enough to use. Sheets had been hung over the inside of the windows and a rusted hulk of a car sat on blocks off to one side. It was not a very inviting place to be. I wondered if Donna ever visited her daughter here.

"I don't know, Tommi," Frank said. "Those stairs don't look too safe. Let me try them first."

"Don't be silly," I told him. "You're heavier than I am. Besides, you can't afford to get hurt. You've got to be healthy to take care of Nina. I'll be very careful."

"Well, go ahead," he said. "Since they haven't collapsed yet under the occupants, they're probably sturdier than they look."

I took them gingerly, and they squeaked and groaned under my weight, but they held. There was no doorbell, so I knocked loudly on the door. I figured the trailer must have been thirty or forty years old, and the door probably hadn't been painted since it was new. Gray as Tee's catnip mouse, it was beginning to splinter.

Finally the door opened a few inches, a chain preventing it from opening further. I could see a blue eye and a bit of hair, a shade of red that has never grown naturally from any human scalp.

"Yeah?"

"Are you Lana Ridenhour?"

"Why do you want to know?"

"My name is Tommi Poag," I told her, assuming

since I didn't get a negative response it must be Lana. "I'd like to talk to you about your father, if I may. And please accept my condolences."

She let out a snort. "No need for that. My dad and I weren't close. What do you want to talk about?"

"I'm working for the lawyer who represents the man accused of killing him. I'm doing some background investigation, and it would be very helpful if you would talk to me."

"How did you find me?"

"I talked with your mother. She gave me your address."

Lana closed the door and I thought she was ending our conversation, but she was sliding the chain off its hook. She opened it wide. Then she saw Frank standing to the side of the steps. "And who's that?"

"His name is Frank Poag. He's helping me."

"Oh. He's your husband?"

"No, actually we're not related." I wasn't going to explain that he was first cousin to my ex-husband. It gets too convoluted.

"That's pretty weird. Well, come on in." She nodded for us to enter the living room. I'll have to admit I was surprised when I got inside. While the furniture was obviously old and worn, the place was neat with rather poignant attempts to make it attractive. A drinking glass on a battered coffee table held two red tulips, though I wondered where they came from since there were no flowers in the yard. Thumb-tacked to the wall were photos of gardens, probably cut from an issue of *Better Homes and Gardens* or some other gardening magazine. To cover up what was probably filthy carpeting, a cheap porch rug in blue and green stripes was in the center of the small room with a threadbare brown love seat at the far end and two old wicker chairs facing it. It looked as though she'd covered the chair cushions with green bath towels tucked under the edges. A couple of side tables and cheap but not unattractive lamps completed the décor.

"You wanna sit, go ahead," she said, flopping into one of the chairs.

Frank and I sat side by side on the love seat.

"I understand you live here with your boyfriend," I said. I wanted to learn as much about Lana as she'd let me know. But I thought I would have to tread carefully if I wanted her cooperation.

"Yeah, I do. He's out right now."

"And his name is?" I asked. She apparently wasn't going to volunteer any information.

"I don't think you need to know that." Lana was twirling a piece of her flame red hair around her forefinger and swinging her crossed leg defiantly. I had a hunch she really wasn't such a hard-nosed character, but was protecting an inner fragility with an outer shell of phony toughness. Having Fulton as a father would be enough to drive anyone to shield her true feelings.

"Okay," I agreed. I figured he probably owned this ramshackle trailer and I could find his name through public records. Then perhaps Bernard could find out if he had a criminal record. There was a slim possibility that her boyfriend was so angry he decided to kill Fulton because he turned Lana down when she asked for money. Since Donna was the sole beneficiary of his estate, the boyfriend wouldn't have killed Fulton for what Lana would inherit. Unless, of course, the couple assumed she was in the will.

"Could I ask you some questions about your father then?"

"I suppose so. But I don't know what good it will do. I left home a few years back. Haven't seen him all that much."

"Your mom told me you'd gone to see him a couple of times to ask him for money."

She gave me a quirky grin. "Yeah. That was a big mistake."

"Why do you say that?"

"It gave him a chance to tell me what a loser I am again. He was very good at that."

It took me a minute to speak. I was afraid my voice would break. "I'm sorry," I said. And I meant that very sincerely.

Lana shrugged. "That was my dad. I should have known better than to go over there." She worked very hard at being stoic.

Frank had sat quietly without comment. But Lana's situation had obviously touched him. "I have three daughters myself, Lana. Parents try very hard to do the right thing. But you know, we're all just human. Sometimes we say and do things that are hurtful thinking we're saying them for their benefit."

Lana's eyes blazed. "You didn't know my dad. He was just one mean son of a bitch."

Frank looked shocked. Chastised, he sat back and said nothing more.

"I had only met your father recently," I said. "I live in the same complex he did. Did you know about the lawsuit he brought against the condo association?"

She snorted again. It seemed to be her way of dealing with the topic of her father.

"Yeah, Mom told me about that. What a farce! Dad really hated dogs, you know. The only reason he took Marty when Grandma died was 'cause he thought he could make big bucks out of him. That was good old dad—anything for a buck! He kept him in that dog cage most of the time, poor thing. I wouldn't put it past him to have set it up so the dog could get out when the painters came. Just so he could sue you guys. Probably thought he could make more money with less fuss that way than doing the dog show thing."

"Your mother suggested the same thing to me. Do you think he and his neighbor were in cahoots over leaving out the antifreeze?"

"Naw. Dad talked about how he hated his neighbors. Called them losers. Said he let Marty dump in their yards just for the fun of it."

A new idea occurred to me. "Didn't he have a trainer for Sir Martingale? Someone who got him ready for the shows?"

"Oh, sure. You don't think he was going to mess with Marty that much himself, do you?"

"Do you know who it was?"

"Some lady down in Asheboro. She took Marty home for a few weeks after Dad first got him to train him, and she'd take him around to the shows. I don't think Dad liked to have to pay her. Another reason he'd want to find another way to make money out of Marty."

"Do you happen to know her name?"

"Nope."

I figured if I needed to talk with her, it wouldn't be too difficult to find her.

Frank stood up. "Do you mind if I use your bathroom?" he asked.

Lana pointed toward the hall. "First door on the right."

I was just as glad he was leaving the room. I didn't think Lana would want to talk about her father's sex life in front of a man. But then, who knows? Sex is not the taboo subject it was for our generation. When I was young, we might have gossiped about it with our best friends, but we didn't talk about it openly with strangers.

"Lana, I understand your father might have been involved with some woman. But she was only seen going into his place at night, as if they were trying to hide it. Do you know anything about that?"

"I don't know who it was, if that's what you mean. I did see some cosmetics in the bathroom while I was over there. And a woman's robe hung on the back of the door."

"Did you ask him about it?"

"Sure. I was curious."

"And what did he say?"

"He said it was none of my damn business. I don't know why I expected anything different from him."

Lana was slumped in her chair now; it seemed the more we talked about her father, the more the steam went out of her. I felt in a way I was torturing the poor girl, though that wasn't my intention. I could only think of one last question to ask her.

"Do you know of anyone in particular who might have wanted to see your father dead?"

"Frankly, half the world hated his guts. But I can't think of anyone who hated him that much. He just liked to screw everyone over. But not to the extent it would lead to his murder. At least I don't think so."

I heard the toilet flush and Frank came back into the living room. I stood up to go. "We really appreciate your help, Lana. Here's my card. If you think of anything, please give me a call."

Logan had given me business cards that said "Tommi Poag, Administrative Assistant, Stewardship Life." It had my work number and I'd written in my home and cell phones as well. I'd used the cards only once or twice, but decided they could be very useful now.

Lana dragged herself out of her chair. She took the

card and stuck it in her pocket. "Can't imagine that I would think of anything else."

"Well, just in case. Thanks for your time."

I left the trailer and noticed Frank waited till I got to the bottom of the stairs until he stepped on them, afraid the two of us might send them crashing.

"You were sure quiet," I said after we got in the car and started back down the rutted driveway.

"I'm just getting the feel of it," he said. "Don't know enough yet to add much to the conversation."

"Just ask whatever comes into your mind. You might think of something that I don't."

"Well, I did find something that might be helpful."

"What's that?"

We were turning back onto Route 61 now and I was glad to be off that terrible bumpy path. My bones felt like I'd been on some wild carnival ride. My frame isn't as hardy as it once was.

"I glanced into one of the bedrooms and saw that a computer was on. Apparently Lana had been on it when you knocked on the door and hadn't bothered to click it off. The screen saver was on, but a little swish of the mouse brought up the screen she'd been looking at."

"Don't keep me in suspense. What was it?"

"It was eBay."

"What's so strange about that?"

"It's just that she doesn't appear to have the money to buy things from eBay. And I'm talking about things like the nice lighting fixtures that were on the screen."

"Maybe she's selling stuff?"

"Like what? I didn't see one thing that she could get two bucks for. Except for the computer of course. Wonder how she afforded that? Looks like a new model."

THIRTEEN

WE WENT TO LUNCH at Panera's on Lawndale. I ordered my perennial favorite, chicken noodle soup with a big hunk of whole wheat bread, and Frank had a Portobello and mozzarella Panini sandwich.

"So what's next?" Frank asked as we finished up our meals.

"I was wondering if you'd like to go see Bernard. I could give him an update on all my interviews. And I think you should be the one to tell him about Nina."

"You're right," Frank said. "I've been so wrapped up in her problems that I hadn't thought to contact Bernard. He'll want to know."

Frank drove us downtown to the offices of Carruther, Mierjeski and Poag on Greene Street near the recently erected statue of General Nathanael Greene. It had been commissioned as part of the Bicentennial celebration and is an elegant eleven-foot-tall figure on a ten-foot-high marble platform that does Greene and Greensboro proud. It stands majestically in the center of the new traffic circle at the corner of Greene and McGee. Bernard's office is just north of there in the heart of downtown.

A receptionist greeted us who must have been a temporary because I hadn't seen her before. She was young, pretty, and visibly nervous. I figured she was not long out of school.

"It's Tommi and Frank Poag here to see Mr. Poag," I said.

She looked a little bewildered at that. Since Bernard's wife Pam also works there, that was a lot of Poags floating around. The girl would have no idea I was Bernard's ex-wife and no relation at all to Frank.

"Just a minute, please," she said, and called back to Bernard's secretary. Within a few minutes we were ushered into his office.

Bernard rose, smiling, his hand outstretched. "Hello, Tommi. And Frank, good to see you. What are you doing in town?"

What a difference a couple of years can make. When I first met Frank he was shouting obscenities at Bernard that he dare try to represent Nina when she was accused of killing her husband. Their hatred of each other was palpable then. Thank God that was all behind them. We sat in the two chairs across from his desk.

"I'm afraid it's not good news," Frank said, sitting down. "It's Nina. She's been diagnosed with breast cancer."

Bernard's smile vanished. "Oh, no. My God I'm sorry to hear that. Has she had surgery?"

"It's scheduled for tomorrow. I've decided to transfer

back to Greensboro, Bernard. I don't know how long Nina will need me, but I want to be here for her."

"That's good, Frank. I'm glad to hear that. And let me know anything I can do. Will she be in the hospital for long?"

"It's done as outpatient surgery."

"Unbelievable," Bernard said. "That's our health system for you. Well, let me know when I can visit her at home." He turned to me. "How's it going with you, Tommi? Anything to report yet?"

"I've done several interviews," I said. "Not that it's pointed me in any special direction. But each person I talk to adds just a little more information so it's picking up speed." I went on to describe my talks with Fulton's neighbors, past and present, his ex-wife and daughter. I told him what additional information Joe Kernodle had given me as well.

"So Joe Kernodle, the guy who threatened him and forced him to withdraw the lawsuit, says he was fishing on Sunday?"

"That's what he says. I don't see how I can check it out."

"It'll be damn near impossible to verify since he goes fishing alone."

"I know," I said. "But, you know, Bernard, it seems to me Fulton had more reason to want to murder Joe than the other way around. Joe was pretty puffed up over getting the better of Fulton. Why would he want to kill him?"

"That's always the question, isn't it?"

"The ultimate one."

"Maybe I could check up on the fact that someone snitched on Ridenhour when he was taking the bar exam," Bernard said. "Kind of strange that he took it twice and failed before someone alerted the local bar that he'd cheated in Missouri. I might be able to find out who that was."

"I don't know if it will help, but it couldn't hurt. The more we find out who was on Fulton's radar, the better."

"Speaking of radar, what's your take on the fact some woman was seen sneaking into Ridenhour's house at night?"

"Since he was single, she wasn't being covert on his account. So I figure it must be some married woman. But I'll be darned if I can figure out who."

"What about his daughter's boyfriend? You said she wouldn't tell you his name? That seems a little odd."

"She must be hiding something. Can't you find out who it is through the Register of Deeds as long as you know where he lives?"

"As a matter of fact I can do it online. What's the address?"

I gave it to him and he spent a few minutes typing away at his computer. "Here it is. Herman James is the name. Let me see if he has a record."

Bernard started typing again. I knew I should get a computer for home. I'd avoided it so far since I had one at work, figuring I could look up anything I wanted to there. But that left me with no access when I wasn't at the office.

"Aha," he said. "He is in the system. Nothing big: petty theft, vandalism, several traffic violations."

"Nothing violent?"

"No. I don't know if it's worth pursuing. I'll leave it up to you."

"I'll keep him on my list. I believe he repairs motorcycles. I could probably track him down that way if I decide to. One thing is for sure."

"What's that?"

"He doesn't go by Herman."

Both men laughed at that, nodding agreement.

"So what's next, Tommi?" Bernard asked.

"I thought I'd talk to Bob Hayes's wife. They're the neighbors who moved away the day after the murder."

"But you don't think they had anything to do with it."

"Not really. I'd just like to hear what she has to say. Oh, and I forgot to tell you. Rhonda Worthington, the president of the condo association, gave me a call this morning. Donna Ridenhour had phoned her and told her that Fulton never got around to changing his will. Donna inherits the condo and everything in it."

"From what you've told me about Ridenhour, it sounds like she deserves everything she gets."

"She sure does. But she told Rhonda she didn't want any of the stuff inside the house and wants to donate it to the homeowners' association to do what they want with it. Rhonda has asked me to take an inventory and make plans for a yard sale. This is perfect because it gives me a chance to get inside and look around."

Bernard smiled. "Looks like Lady Luck is on your side today. Of course the police no doubt went through it and took anything that might help in their case."

"That's the point, Bernard. They're building a different case than we are. So there might be something helpful to us that they overlooked."

"When are you going to do this?"

"In the morning, if I can get the key."

"Good girl." Imagine Bernard saying this to me. I felt like I'd gone through the looking glass to Wonderland.

I rose and Frank followed suit. "We won't take up any more of your time," I said.

Bernard turned to Frank. "All right if I call Nina tonight?"

"Please do," he said. "It would mean a lot to her."

SHIRLEY AND BOB Hayes had moved to a little rental house on Northwood Street. Northwood runs off of Battleground Avenue somewhat parallel to Wendover Avenue, a main artery that meanders from the east side of town to the southwest. Except for a few blocks downtown, very few streets in Greensboro are parallel to one another. The town has grown like Topsy, with streets sometimes changing names every few blocks as growth spurts caused separate roads to be joined, hence the shift in name. Even longtime residents have trouble finding their way around at times.

They now lived in a square white-clapboard ranch that couldn't have been more than a thousand square feet. I wondered how they even managed that since they no doubt had to make mortgage payments on their condo until it sold, and Shirley didn't work because of her illness. It had to be a very difficult situation for them.

I'd called Shirley on my cell phone when we left Bernard's office and asked if we could come.

"If you'll excuse the mess," she said. "I'm working slowly on getting settled, but it's going to take a while."

"That won't matter to us in the least," I assured her.

When I rang the bell, Shirley, a tall, thin woman, taller I suspect than her husband, opened the door. She had on blue jeans and a sweatshirt that said UNCG, the local university that is part of the University of North Carolina system. Her long brown hair hung very straight and fell over her shoulders, and her brown eyes looked tired.

I introduced myself and Frank and said, "I hope you don't mind us bothering you. I know how busy you must be."

"Please, come in. I'm always looking for an excuse to take a break." We followed her into the tiny living room. I noticed she walked with a slight limp and her body seemed stiff, as if it was painful to move. Furniture was scattered helter-skelter, and boxes were piled high along the back wall. I could see into the small kitchen beyond where stacks of dishes and pots and pans covered the countertops and a drop leaf kitchen table. Crumpled newspaper was overflowing a large plastic garbage can dominating the center of the room, next to a large open carton still half full of newspaper-wrapped breakables.

"Can I get you a Coke or something?" she asked as she indicated for us to sit on the yellow-flowered sofa. She sat in a matching wing-back chair.

"Thanks, no," I said. "I just want to ask a few questions, and then we'll get out of your hair." I explained why I was there.

"I don't know Garland Merritt," she said. "But from what you've said, it sounds like the police have the wrong man."

"I feel sure of it. And since you lived next door to Fulton, I hoped you might be able to give me your take on the man. He seemed to be quite a controversial figure."

I could see a shudder run through her. "He was despicable. He frightened my husband so badly we felt we had to move."

"This was because of the dog dying."

"Oh, yes. That was the final straw. We'd had a number of run-ins with him, but when his dog died, he threatened Bob with bodily harm." She closed her eyes and shook her head at the thought of it.

"And that's why you moved."

"Of course. I don't know if my husband told you or not, but I have MS. And stress just makes the symptoms worse. I was a basket case living next door to that monster."

"Mrs. Hayes…"

"Please, it's Shirley."

"I want you to know that what I'm going to tell you is just conjecture. It might not be true at all. But I've had a couple of people tell me that they think Fulton planned to have his dog run away. That he might have wanted to collect the insurance on him."

Shirley's mouth fell open a little. "He planned it?"

"I don't know that for a fact. But these people think that when the dog drank from the pan of antifreeze, it was purely a coincidence."

She looked as though she couldn't comprehend what I was saying to her. "I…I don't get it. That doesn't make sense. If he wanted the dog to escape, why would he threaten us? Did it matter to him whether the dog simply ran away or died?"

I could see that Frank was puzzled too. "What are you saying, Tommi? Do you think those people might be right? Surely this guy wasn't broken up over the fact his dog died if he'd wanted it to run away."

I'd been thinking about Fulton and the Hayeses on the drive from downtown. And a new thought had occurred to me. Did I want to share it? Would they think I'd lost my mind?

I must have been staring into space because I heard Frank say, "Tommi?"

"I'm working on a theory here. Knowing what kind of an SOB Fulton was, I'm wondering if it's true he planned on the dog escaping. If so, when the dog drank the antifreeze and died, that led to a whole new possibility for him to swindle somebody else. Shirley, he knew about your illness, didn't he?"

"Oh, sure. He even made a mean-spirited joke or two about the way I walk."

"What a great guy," Frank said bitterly, looking as though he wished Fulton were still around so he could punch him out.

"Okay, so here's my thought. What if he decided he'd stumbled onto the golden opportunity. He'd accomplished his mission: to get rid of the dog. But now he could intimidate you guys as well. He realized if he put enough pressure on you, you'd probably move out, especially since you can't deal with that kind of stress. In this awful housing market, he figured you'd be willing to sell the house dirt cheap just to get out from under the mortgage. Then he could buy it and flip it for profit. He could afford to wait the market out, maybe rent it out for a while, and eventually sell it for a much better price."

I was feeling pretty proud of my clever scenario until Shirley broke down into sobs. Then I realized how hard that must have hit her. I had been unconsciously cruel to her. Both Frank and I jumped up and went over to her, trying to calm her down.

"Shirley, Shirley," I said, taking her hand. "I don't know if it's true or not. I was just trying to come up with possibilities."

Frank went into the kitchen and got her a glass of

water. "Here, drink this," he said kindly. She wiped her eyes with the backs of both hands and grasped the glass taking several swallows.

She seemed a little calmer now. "I'm sorry. I was so upset about this move. I didn't want to leave our home. And it just sounds so much like what he would do, I think you're right."

"But, you know what?" I said. "Fulton didn't get a chance to act on it. You could still move back into your house."

Tears started to run down Shirley's face again. "I'm just too exhausted. I couldn't face another move. Even back there as much as I want to go."

Frank had been standing over her keeping a close watch. I think he was worried about her reaction and how it was affecting her health.

"Did you sign a long lease on this house?" he asked. "Or are you on a month-to-month basis?"

"It's monthly. Why?" she asked.

"Why don't you plan to spend the rest of the month here. Don't unpack any more than you have to. Then Tommi and I will organize a bunch of your former neighbors to move you back into your old home. You can just relax and take it easy. And, of course, take your house off the market in the meantime."

She looked at him in amazement. "I can't let you do that!"

"Why ever not?" I asked. "I know that the board members would love to help. You know, we can't let

Fulton get the last laugh here. We've got to make sure that he can't reach from beyond the grave to screw someone over one final time."

Shirley shook her head. "I'm speechless."

FOURTEEN

WHEN SHIRLEY WAS ASSURED we meant what we said, she seemed overwhelmed with gratitude and actually smiled. "Of course I'll have to talk to Bob about it," she said, wiping away tears of gratitude this time, "but I can't imagine that he would say no. He hated leaving our place as much as I did. We loved everything about it except Fulton Ridenhour. And of course he'd want to help with the move."

"We'll put him to work then, and we'll send you off to a spa for the full treatment," I said. "We'll plan it for a weekend so he won't have to take any more time off work. Now, do you mind if I ask you a few more questions?"

"Of course not. Right now I'd kiss your feet if you asked me to."

Frank laughed. "I think she'd settle for a hug."

Shirley got up stiffly, came over and put her arms around me. "Consider yourself hugged," she said. Then she embraced Frank, and he patted her on the back.

Once she was settled back in the chair I asked her

if she'd ever seen anyone sneaking into Fulton's place.

"You know, I have. I don't always sleep well at night, and sometimes when I was restless I would go sit in the living room in the dark so I wouldn't bother Bob."

"So what did you see?"

"Several times I saw a car pull up in front of his place and someone get out and hurry up to the front door. She never had to knock, but would go right in like it was left open for her."

"You say she," I said. "Are you sure it was a woman?"

Shirley thought for a moment. "Well, no. It was too dark to tell. But why would a man sneak in at night?"

"Knowing Fulton, any kind of skullduggery is possible. Could you see what kind of a car it was?"

"Again, it was hard to tell at night. But it looked like an old Ford we used to have."

"What color was it?"

"Something dark. That's all I know."

That confirmed what Bob had said. "Did Bob ever see that happening?" I wondered if they'd been together or had seen it on separate occasions.

"I don't know. He was never up when I saw it."

So they'd seen the car at different times. That meant the person had been at Fulton's fairly often.

"Had that been going on for very long?"

"It's been a while. Can't remember when I first saw her. Or him."

I was running out of ideas. "Anything you want to

ask her, Frank?" I knew he held back because I was
the one Bernard hired, and he didn't want to horn in.
But two minds are always better than one.

"I was wondering if Ridenhour had any relation-
ships before this secretive one. Had there been any
women to his house prior to that? Openly, I mean."

"Yes, I'd seen several different women coming and
going from his house since he moved in. None of
them seemed to care whether anyone saw them or not.
I'll have to say they seemed like a sleazy looking
bunch."

"Had any of those women been around since this
mystery person started coming?" Frank asked.

"No, come to think of it, not that I saw," Shirley
said.

I could tell Shirley was tiring under our question-
ing. I gave her one of my business cards and told her
to call me if she thought of anything else.

"And we'll get back to you soon to set up a
moving day," Frank said. "I even think I know where
I can borrow a truck so there won't be that expense.
And we'll get a team over here the day before to
repack things. We don't want you to lift a finger."

Shirley's eyes welled up again. "I don't know how
to thank you. This is the nicest thing anyone has ever
done for us."

"It's about time something nice happened to you,"
I said. "You've had enough bad luck lately."

As we left the house Frank told her, "And don't

forget to call your Realtor and take your place off the market."

She hugged us both again.

FRANK DECIDED it was time for him to go back to Nina's house. "I think she should be through with all the tests by now. She's probably getting pretty nervous."

"Can I go with you?"

"She didn't get much sleep last night. I'm going to suggest that she lie down for a while."

"How about if I come this evening and bring you dinner?"

"You must have been reading my mind. I don't want her to cook, and I didn't think she'd want to go out. But, you know, I'm one hell of a crappy chef."

I laughed. "Haven't you realized all this time since you've known me that I'm just as lousy a cook as you are? But there's always take-out. What would you prefer? Chinese? Italian? Mexican? None of the above?"

"Why don't you surprise us."

I agreed to do that and he took me back to my place.

"Sevenish okay?" I asked.

"Perfect," he said and drove off.

IT WAS THREE-THIRTY and I didn't know what I could accomplish before going to Oak Ridge since I'd have to pick up dinner on the way. I decided I could make some phone calls if nothing else. In the notes I had made to myself I'd jotted down the fact that Fulton's dog handler lived in Asheboro. Surely there couldn't be too many dog trainers there since the town has only about twenty thousand inhabitants.

I suddenly remembered meeting a woman involved in dog shows when I recently had lunch with a friend at a retirement community called Pennybyrn in High Point. Years ago she and her late husband had begun a business as show superintendents, which meant they handled the arrangements to put on hundreds of dog shows throughout the country. This was before I knew about Fulton Ridenhour and his dog or I would have asked many more questions. But I'd found it pretty fascinating at the time.

I phoned my friend Lib for the number then called Lois Crowe who owns MBF Incorporated in Greensboro. She told me how to reach a professional handlers' association who could give me that information. Fortunately they were able to give me the name of the only English Spaniel trainer in Asheboro. I love networking; it makes getting information so much easier.

Mary Lee Baumgartner answered the phone with a syrupy-sweet Southern drawl. "Yee-esss?" she inquired, making the word two syllables.

I introduced myself and told her why I was calling in some detail.

"Oh, my goodness! You don't mean to tell me that Sir Martingale is day-ed!! What a tragedy!"

I noticed she remarked on the death of the dog but not on Fulton. How strange was that?

"Yes, it was a very unfortunate accident." I didn't bother to tell her that we thought Fulton had meant for the dog to escape.

"Oh, he was the sweetest thing. I simply loved that dawg."

"I understand that you kept him for a while to train him and have been taking him to dog shows since then."

"Well, I used to."

"Used to? What do you mean?" Of course I realized it was odd that she didn't already know about the dog's death. Obviously she hadn't been able to take him to shows for the last three or four weeks. Did they have grace periods between shows so the dog could rest? Having watched a few Westminster shows on television, I would have thought the trainers needed more rest than the dogs, the way they ran them around the ring.

"I told Fulton last month I wouldn't work with him any more."

Now that was news. "Why is that?"

"I didn't think he treated that precious dog right. And I didn't want to be a part of it."

"Did he abuse him in some way?"

"Not so I could call authorities on him or anything like that. After all, Fulton expected to make money off him once he retired from dog shows so he couldn't physically hurt him. But he hollered at him all the time. Never said a kind word. And I know he kept him in the cage way too much. I just felt the man didn't want to be bothered with him except for the money end. If an owner doesn't love his pet, I won't work with him. Animals are just like humans; they need love. And there was no love at all in that house. I was hoping that if I quit, maybe he'd give the dog away to someone who really cared about him."

No wonder Fulton planned to have the dog run away. Without winning the dog shows, Sir Martingale wouldn't fetch the stud fees he was expecting.

As an afterthought, Mary Lee said, "How did you say Fulton was killed?" This seemed more out of curiosity than any feeling of regret. Join the crowd, Mary Lee.

"He was run through with a sword at the Reenactment of the Battle of Guilford Courthouse."

"Ewwww. That sounds pretty nasty."

"Not a fun way to die, I'm sure. But it was quick."

"Well, I doubt he's going to meet Sir Martingale in heaven. I would suspect he went the other way."

A lot of people seemed to share that thought. "I appreciate your help, Mary Lee," I told her. "By the way, I expect you have a busy schedule. I find what you do very interesting. Do you have to go to shows every weekend?" Just thought I'd find out whether she could have been in Greensboro the past Sunday with an urge to kill the man who was so mean to his dog.

"You betcha. I haven't had a weekend free for months. Was up in New Jersey this last weekend. But

I love all these babies I work with so much, I wouldn't have it any other way."

That seemed easy enough to verify, though I felt very strongly that Mary Lee had nothing to do with Fulton's death.

After I hung up, I remembered Rhonda's call to me about Fulton's house. Perhaps she'd gotten the key by now, and I could get inside a take a look around. The word around the association was that Rhonda had inherited some money and didn't need to work. That gave her plenty of time to run the homeowners' association like an autocrat and micro-manage everything. I'd heard that before her mother died and left her a nice inheritance, Rhonda had been administrative assistant to one of the well-known CEOs in town, and had brought her brusque style of management to the board. There was no doubt she could get things done. It was the way she did them that had everyone so riled up.

I called Rhonda's number and it rang and rang. Well, darn. I was staring out the front window wondering what to do next when I saw Rhonda striding down the sidewalk. Speak of coincidence!

I had the door open when she got to my steps.

"Hi, Rhonda. Come on in."

She swished into my living room and looked around with a rather jaundiced eye. I'm sure my décor didn't meet up with her standards.

"Won't you have a seat?" I asked.

"No, no. I'm on my way to do another errand. I just got the key to Fulton's place off his wife and I wanted to drop it by." She handed me a small envelope. "Now if you could do an inventory and make a report to the board at our meeting next week, we can proceed from there. We mainly need to know what there is of value and how much simply needs to be discarded."

"What about appliances?" I asked.

"The stove usually stays with the house when it's sold. But we could sell the refrigerator and laundry equipment."

"Okay, Rhonda. I'll do it as soon as I can. I'm going to visit a friend this evening who's having surgery tomorrow. But I can probably do it in the morning."

"Fine," she said abruptly and left.

I decided the only thing I had time to do was take a little breather before going to Oak Ridge. So I indulged myself by taking a long, hot soak in a tub full of wonderful bergamot mint aromatherapy oils. Crazy Tee stood with his front paws on the edge of the tub, batting occasionally at the little ripples of oil that floated on the surface. If cats were supposed to loathe water, no one ever told him that.

AFTER MY BATH I decided to order carry-out from Lucky 32 restaurant on Westover Terrace, a sister restaurant to the Print Works Bistro. The food would be superior, and I wanted something special for Frank and Nina even though it would put a dent in my food budget for the week. I ordered three dinners of Carolina catfish with grits and seasonal vegetables with lemon chess pie for dessert. I ordered a nice bottle of chardonnay as well. Nina usually worried about her figure, but I hoped that tonight she would take a pass.

I drove over to pick it up a little after six and headed out to Nina's house which is in Oak Ridge, a small town northwest of Greensboro at the intersection of Highways 68 and 150. Nina's house was a little way out of town and, in an area of fine large homes, stood apart as the biggest and showiest of all. It wasn't Nina who'd wanted such an expensive and prestigious home, it had been her late husband Cap, or Oscar, as he had been christened. Cap had been a successful scriptwriter with big budget movies and an Oscar nomination to his credit, and when they moved from California to North Carolina, he'd wanted to impress. And impress he did. Now she rattled around in the oversized mansion by herself. She wanted desperately to sell it, but with the housing market gone to hell, her chances of doing so any time soon were slim. It was a good thing she inherited enough money for the upkeep.

The house was perched on the top of a small round hill surrounded by a number of huge oak trees. The land had originally been the site of an old farm house, but had been purchased some years earlier by a man who lived in a modest home near the Oak Ridge Academy. He'd made a fortune in tech stocks and built the house to please his wife when their daughter was getting married. She'd wanted a beautiful setting for the wedding and reception.

Unfortunately his wife died a year or so after they moved in, and he lost the will to live, following her in death a few months later. It was such a pricey house that few in the area could afford it. Since Cap sold his California home at the height of the extravagant real estate boom there, he could well afford to buy the most expensive house around.

The exterior had a strong resemblance to Tara, and I'd always wondered if the fact that Cap was in the movie business had influenced his purchase of the home. A two-story high porch spread across the entire front of the house, and Nina had furnished it with wrought iron chairs and benches with intricate scrolls and flourishes.

I gathered the bag of food and the bottle of wine out of the car and struggled to make it to the front door without fumbling them.

Nina answered the doorbell and took the bottle of wine out of my hands before I lost my grip. "Wow," she said, "I didn't expect this. What else have you got? You must not have Subways if you're bringing wine."

"A surprise," I said. "You'll have to wait and see."

I followed her down the hall which led between the living and dining rooms furnished with exquisite Williamsburg-era antiques in a palette of pastels. The family room at the rear of the house was much more casual with oversized down-filled chairs and matching sofa in a Carolina Blue that matched the cloudless sky seen through the two-story glass wall at the back. French doors led out onto a deck and pool, but it was much too cool yet to sit outside. The woods beyond were beginning to show a hint of the yellow and green of budding leaves. This was the room she lived in.

Frank was sitting on the sofa and stood up to take the boxes from my hands. "Here, you two visit. I'll dish this up onto plates," he said. He took the bottle from Nina and disappeared into the kitchen.

Nina and I settled into chairs across from the sofa.

"How did it go today?" I asked her.

"Oh, you know, they have to make sure you're alive and breathing before they operate on you. I had to fill out questionnaires and go through a bunch of tests. I just want to get it over with. It's the anticipation that's so awful."

"What time is your surgery tomorrow?"

"Eight a.m. That means I have to be there at six. You know I usually don't get up till nine in the morning. What a bummer."

I shook my head. "When they say eight, they probably mean nine. They'll leave you lying there with IVs in your arm and feeling like you have to pee your pants. Except you won't have pants on."

She laughed. "I know. You can never produce when they want you to, but when you can't get up, that's when you have to go."

We had a good laugh over that. I was so glad her sense of humor was still intact.

Frank stuck his head around the corner and said, "Soup's on. Come and get it."

He'd laid out the breakfast table with festive orange

place mats and flowered napkins and had dished the meal onto Nina's best china. The bottle of wine was open and sitting in an ice bucket on the counter and goblets at each place glistened from the overhead light.

"Oh, that looks good," Nina said. "What kind of fish is that?"

"Catfish," I said. "Carolina catfish."

"My favorite," she enthused. I loved doing things for Nina, She always appreciates whatever you do for her.

As we sat down, Frank said, "Do you mind if I say a blessing?"

Both Nina and I said "of course not," simultaneously.

I was surprised. Frank is not an outwardly religious person. We bowed our heads and he said, "Heavenly father, bless this food, and bless my daughter that she will be safe in your loving hands tomorrow. And bless Tommi for her friendship that means so much to both of us. Amen."

I was so touched I had to surreptitiously wipe a tear from the corner of my eye.

We chatted about weather, current events, even politics on which we thankfully agreed, anything to avoid discussing that elephant in the room: the surgery. I had a feeling that Nina was not mentioning it for Frank's sake. Since her mother had died of breast cancer, it had to be doubly hard for him.

We all cleaned our plates of every last morsel, and

almost finished off the pie, both Nina and I ignoring our usual caution when it came to calories. I seemed to have been doing that a lot in recent days.

"Oh, Tommi, what a treat," Nina said when we were done. "Thank you so much."

"I'm just sorry I'm not a gourmet cook who could whip you up a fabulous meal, but I thought you might appreciate something other than Lean Cuisine."

"You two go back to the family room," Frank said, "and let me clear up. I'll be with you in a minute."

When he came back into the room, Nina said, "Okay, now, you guys. I want to hear all about your day."

We took turns telling her about our interviews with Lana Ridenhour, Bernard, and Shirley Hayes.

"Aw, Dad, that's sweet what you told Shirley," Nina said. "I'd like to help move her too."

"We'll see, we'll see," he said. I knew he worried about whether she would feel up to it if she was undergoing treatment.

"I'm sure the whole homeowners' board will help," I said. "There was no love lost for Fulton with that group. I think they'd want to make things right."

I told them about my phone call to Mary Lee Baumgartner and the fact she'd quit handling Fulton's dog.

"Well, that cinches it in my mind," Frank said. "I feel sure now he wanted that dog to get out."

"Maybe I'll find some evidence for that. I've got the key to his place, and I'm going over there tomorrow morning to see what I can learn."

FIFTEEN

I WOKE UP AT SEVEN when Tee pounced on my stomach and began to whine in his feline way. I knew his food bowl must be empty. I dragged myself out of bed, thinking of Nina at the Outpatient Surgery clinic, wondering if she was calm or scared. I knew I was scared for her. Frank wouldn't let me sit with him in the waiting room.

"You've got work to do," he'd insisted. "Bernard's counting on you to come up with some helpful information. Go do your thing." No amount of persuasion could sway him. I'd made him promise to call me on my cell phone as soon as the surgery was over.

I filled Tee's bowl, ate my usual Honey Bunches of Oats with bananas on top and drank an extra cup of coffee hoping the caffeine would give me the extra jolt I needed to get going. Before I dressed, I touched base with Constance and assured her I was making progress. I only wished I felt as positive as I tried to pretend.

I dressed in blue jeans and sweatshirt figuring the heat might be off in Fulton's house or at least turned down to a minimum. I gathered up a legal pad, pens and calculator to take with me with the vague notion of adding up guesstimates of what the items in his house could bring in a yard sale. I'd been a yard sale prowler in my younger days, not so much for the bargains but the thrill of the hunt. I quit when I realized I'd been bringing home stuff I didn't need or couldn't possibly use. I think I did it partly because Bernard always worked on Saturdays, and it gave me something to do other than watch the cartoon network. He was the one who convinced me the articles piling up in the closets and garage had to go. But I had gained some knowledge of how to price items for a sale.

When I unlocked the door of Fulton's house, I found the temperature to be very warm and the smell of something rotting was almost overwhelming. I knew I couldn't work there until I found out what it was and got rid of it. But first I opened the downstairs windows, left the front door open, and used a Kleenex I'd stuck in my pocket to cover my nose. A check of the thermostat showed it was set at eighty degrees. I was going to roast in my sweatshirt so I turned it down to sixty-five. After dropping my purse and legal pad on the coffee table, I followed the odor to the kitchen. There were dirty dishes in the sink, and the countertop was cluttered with what looked like bills, junk mail, and empty fast food containers, but no smelly leftovers. I checked inside the refrigerator, and although some of the food there looked a little worse for wear, I sniffed each container and was sure none of them was responsible for the horrible odor. The thought that I was going to have to clean the fridge out if we were going to sell it was depressing. It was one of the tasks I loathed doing at home.

I looked through the upper cupboards. There was a stack of mismatched dishes, a bunch of jelly glasses, and boxes of cereal and instant potatoes, ramen noodles, and other quickie meals. The only food I found that wasn't packaged was a loaf of moldy bread. A sniff test indicated it didn't smell very good but certainly wasn't the culprit.

The lower cabinets yielded only beat up pans and skillets, an ancient toaster, and a host of liquor bottles. There were cleaning supplies under the sink, though from the look of the place, they'd been used sparingly. I was about to give up entirely, wondering how I could manage to do my search while breathing that ghastly odor, when an idea occurred to me. One of the places in my own house that's always neglected is the space behind the fridge. Even though most refrigerators have wheels so they can be pulled out for cleaning, it seems too much trouble, so the dust puppies grow and flourish there. I wondered if something odorous was lurking behind Fulton's refrigerator.

His model was smaller than most, and by grasping the sides and inching first one side forward then the other, I managed to pull it a few inches into the room. It sat at the end of the counter which allowed me to go around to the left and peer into the dark recesses behind it. I switched on the overhead light to see better and finally found the culprit. There, lying in the middle of greasy looking balls of dust and dirt was a mousetrap with the body of a very large decaying mouse. I gagged and stepped back, knowing I'd have to get rid of it if I was going to be able to stay there. The rodent had probably died a couple of days earlier and had been putrefying ever since. It made me wonder how homicide cops ever dealt with dead bodies. I couldn't even deal with a poor dead mouse.

I looked around for something I could use to extract the trap from behind the fridge. After pulling a trash bag from a box under the sink to dump the trap mouse and all in, I plucked a soiled kitchen towel off the counter to throw over it so I could pick it up without touching it. Then I remembered seeing a yardstick propped in the corner of the dining area. Perfect! I could scoot the trap out from behind the fridge with that. I gathered everything together and began to manipulate the mousetrap toward me with the yardstick.

I had squatted down and had scooted it halfway out by poking at it from behind, when I heard a step behind me. I started to stand up when something hard connected with the side of my head. An explosion of pain sent me reeling sideways and everything went black.

THE FIRST THING I was aware of was that I had a horrendous headache and someone was holding my hand.

I opened my eyes a sliver to prevent the harsh light overhead from adding to my misery and saw the blurry form of Frank to my left. I was lying in a bed, but couldn't figure out whose bed it was. In addition to the throbbing in my head, I realized that there was also a sharp pain in my back somewhere below my right shoulder blade.

"Frank?" I was surprised at how weak my voice sounded.

He leaned over me, squeezing my hand even tighter. "Tommi! Thank God! How are you feeling?" His forehead was creased with anxiety, and he looked as though he'd been up carousing for two whole nights in a row.

I squinted at him. "About as bad as you look. Which is terrible."

"What do you expect when you scare the hell out of me?" He leaned over and kissed me on the cheek. "Welcome back."

"Where have I been?"

"Out cold for about ten hours."

No wonder my head hurt. I tried to remember what had happened. "My head's pounding so much I think my brain is scrambled. Wasn't I at Fulton's house?"

"Before we get into that let me call the nurse and get you something for pain. I think the doctor wants to see you too now that you're awake."

"So which hospital am I in?"

"Moses Cone."

That triggered the memory of Nina's surgery. "How's Nina? Is she okay? Where is she?"

"She's doing well. She's resting at home and a neighbor is there with her."

He refused any further discussion until the medical types checked me all over and gave me some heavy duty medication. The doctor declared I had a mild concussion and I'd have to stay there at least until the next day.

Once I had a pain shot, I knew my time was limited before I zonked out again. I was anxious to find out what happened before I drifted off.

"Tell me, Frank. I'll be asleep again soon, and I want to know what's going on."

"Okay, here's the abbreviated story. We can talk more about it tomorrow when you're feeling better. I tried and tried to reach you when Nina came out of surgery, but I got no answer. Since you were so anxious to hear from me, I knew something was wrong. Thank the good Lord I'd asked for Fulton's address last night. I drove over there while Nina was in recovery, found the door and windows open and you on the floor with blood all over your back."

"Blood? Did my head bleed that much?"

"Your head didn't bleed at all even though you've got a nasty lump. Someone stabbed you in the back."

"Stabbed me!" Shades of Fulton Ridenhour! "What with?"

"It seems to be some kind of a knife. What saved you was it glanced off a rib and didn't hit any vital organ. But it bled like crazy. So your assailant probably thought he'd struck a fatal blow."

I couldn't believe this. It hadn't occurred to me that I was in any danger.

"Who do the police think did it?"

"Right now, Tommi, the theory is someone noticed the door was open, sneaked in to steal something, then saw you and hit you over the head. To make sure you couldn't identify them later, they stabbed you as well. Robberies are turning more lethal these days."

"Now why would the cops think that?"

"Because they stole your keys and your car. And if you had a purse it's gone too."

"Not my Fit! My dear little Fit!"

"They found your car an hour ago. It has some damage to the right front quarter panel, but nothing major."

"Oh, jeez, there goes my year-end bonus I was saving for a getaway weekend this spring." Then another thought occurred to me. "You know what? They have my house key too. To say nothing of my credit cards."

"I'll leave right now and get the locks changed. Do you have a listing of your credit card numbers so I can call it in?"

"In the kitchen drawer to the right of the sink. I keep paperwork in there." I could feel the pain medication beginning to take hold. "I think I need to snooze, now, Frank. Go home and take care of Nina."

He squeezed my hand. "I will, after I get your

locks changed. I'll call about the credit cards from Nina's house. And I'll be back in the morning. The doctor said you could probably be discharged after morning rounds."

I barely heard his final words.

THE NEXT MORNING I was eating scrambled eggs and toast, not quite stone cold, when the phone beside my bed rang.

"It's Bernard," the caller said. "I didn't tell you to try and get yourself killed. What were you thinking, Tommi?"

"I was thinking I was trying to help you out. Getting mugged and stabbed was definitely not in my plans."

"Why on earth would you leave the door open when you were in there alone?"

"Because there was a rotting dead mouse behind the refrigerator, and he stank to high heavens. It was me or the mouse. Both of us could not be in there at the same time." I was so glad to have his sympathy. I damn near get killed and Bernard bawls me out.

"Well, I do worry about you. Take care of yourself, won't you?"

"I'll try to, Bernard."

"Do that," he said. "Anything new you have to tell me?"

Well, at least I got his sympathy for half a minute.

"Remember the next-door neighbor who moved away because of Fulton's threats?"

He paused a minute. "The Hayes family."

"That's the one. Talked to the wife and she con-firmed that someone had been sneaking into Fulton's house at night."

"Could she tell you any more about the person?"

"No. Too dark. I also talked to the woman who handled Fulton's dog. She'd quit working with him a month ago."

"Why?"

"She didn't like the way he treated the dog. No physical abuse, more like neglect. She hoped by quitting he'd give the dog away or sell it to someone who cared."

"That makes it even more probable he wanted the dog to get out."

"That's what I thought."

"Well, be more careful or I'll have to take you off the case."

Gosh. I guess that meant he cared. "Frank told me Nina's doing well."

"Yes, I spoke to her last night. She sounded good."

I wanted to hear all the details, but I didn't think Bernard was the one to discuss it with. So I'd wait till I saw Frank.

After I hung up and the breakfast tray was taken away, a man dressed in brown slacks, a white shirt with a tan striped tie, and a navy windbreaker came in and sat beside my bed. He was movie-star hand-some and reminded me of a young Harry Belafonte.

I wished I'd combed my hair and put on a little lipstick. I felt like the Wicked Witch of the West dressed in a hospital gown. I pulled the sheet and blanket up a little higher to cover whatever unfettered lumps and bumps were obvious.

"I'm Detective Derwin Allred," he said, flashing his badge at me. "I'm here to interview you about the incident yesterday." He flipped open a pad to take notes.

"Okay," I agreed. "Incident" made it sound so benign.

"First of all, what were you doing in that house?"

The cops didn't need to know that I was looking into Fulton's murder. That was between Bernard and me. If I'd been a licensed PI, it might have been different. But I was a private citizen. "The former wife of the man who lived there gave me the key. She had inherited the house." She hadn't given it to me directly but it was almost the same thing.

"Why did she do that?"

"She had bitter memories of her marriage. She wanted to get rid of the furnishings so she could sell the house. But she didn't want to have to go through his stuff."

"So you were doing that for her?"

"I'm a member of the homeowners' association board. We're going to have a yard sale with Mr. Ridenhour's furniture and raise money for our group. I was checking things out to see what was there and what it might be worth."

He took a minute to write that all down. "Okay. How did your assailant get in?"

"There was a dead mouse behind the refrigerator. The smell was bad so I was trying to air out the place, and I'd left the front door open."

"You need to be more careful," he said with genuine concern. "Crime's up with the downturn of the economy, and the bad guys are getting more aggressive. Older women are particularly vulnerable."

"I beg your pardon?" I said miffed.

He smiled sheepishly. "Sorry. Didn't mean to offend."

"I'm not *older*," I said. "I'm *experienced!*"

"Yes, ma'am." The poor man looked like a kid whose mother had just bawled him out for pulling the cat's tail. He took a minute to blow his nose before he resumed his questions. "Did you get a look at your attacker?"

"Not even a glance. I was stooped down trying to get the mousetrap out, and I heard a step behind me. Before I could turn around, I got whacked on the head and knocked out. Did you find the weapons? Do you know what they stabbed me with?"

"No on both counts. The perp must have taken them with him. No fingerprints on the car as well. Must have been wearing gloves."

"So now what?"

"We'll keep on it. We're hoping he tries to use your charge cards. Other than that we haven't much to go on."

"Okay," I shrugged. "Just let me know if you find out anything."

He nodded, shook my hand, and left.

I had to wonder if my attack had anything to do with Fulton's murder or was just a robbery as the police seemed to think.

SIXTEEN

FRANK AND THE DOCTOR arrived at about the same time. The doc, his badge said Dr. Cheng Kim, checked me over thoroughly and pronounced me ready to go home.

"But take it easy for a few days," he said. "And see your own doctor within the week to take a look at the wound on your back. We don't want it to get infected. Sponge baths for a while."

That was the hardest part. I counted on my daily hot soaks to unwind. I would sorely miss them.

Frank handled the process of getting me discharged and went to get his car while the aide bundled me into the wheelchair after helping me get dressed. Since some of the clothing I'd been wearing at the time of the attack was bloody, in fact the sweatshirt and bra had been cut off in the emergency room, I'd asked Frank to get me clean clothes when he got my locks changed. So I had gray slacks and a navy long-sleeve tee shirt along with underclothes to wear. I was well past the point of being embarrassed about having him go through my underwear drawer. He'd brought me a lightweight jacket as well as the temperature had gotten cooler overnight. The jeans and underpants I'd worn when I'd been admitted were rolled up in a plastic bag.

As we pulled out of the hospital parking lot, Frank said, "I'm taking you to Nina's for a couple of days. Even with the locks changed, you shouldn't be home alone."

I assumed he wanted to keep an eye on me because of getting knocked silly more than he worried about me being in my house, but I was anxious to see Nina so I didn't protest.

"So tell me about her," I said.

"Why don't you let her tell you? She'll remember details better than I can."

We rode in companionable silence the rest of the way to Oak Ridge. I'd been given more oral pain medication since my head and back were still hurting, and it put me into a state of languorous dreaminess.

Nina greeted me at the door and hugged me. "Come sit in the family room and put your feet up. How are you feeling?"

"A little loopy right now," I said. "From now on I'm only taking aspirin. The question is how are you?"

"I'm really good, Tommi. I'm feeling very positive."

She led me into the family room and insisted I lie on the couch. She'd already placed a light blanket and down pillow there for me. "Frank went out and brought in something for lunch before he went to the hospital. So you stay right there. He'll help me fix trays for us."

"For Pete's sake, Nina," I protested. "I should be waiting on *you*. I don't need all this pampering."

"Indulge me," she said. "For today at least."

"Okay," I agreed. I had to admit I didn't feel like doing much else. We had a delicious lunch of chicken salad, bunches of green grapes, and wonderful sourdough bread. Nina and I couldn't have wine since we'd both taken pain medication so we toasted our health with ice water.

While Frank cleared up, Nina told me about her surgery. It had turned out that a lumpectomy was sufficient to excise the small malignancy, though she would have to have radiation therapy.

"But the doctor is very optimistic that I'll be okay," she said.

"Oh, Nina," I said and closed my eyes, so relieved that I couldn't speak another word.

She came over and put her arms around me. "I've been bawling over you the past couple of days," she said. "Now that we know we're both going to be all right, we have to thank Whoever is looking over us. We're two lucky gals."

I smiled. "For sure."

The three of us chatted for a while until both Nina and I felt the need for a nap. She took me to the guest bedroom upstairs, furnished with a gorgeous antique canopy bed and dresser. Wall-to-wall white carpeting set off the walnut furniture, and the hand stenciled walls resembling damask in shades of pale green were as soothing as a woodland glade. I couldn't help but think of the contrast between this room and the one at the hospital as I drifted off to sleep.

I AWOKE BEFORE Nina did, and Frank and I sat in the family room and discussed the events of the past couple of days.

"I want to get back into Fulton's house," I said. "I never got a chance to look around."

"Only if I go with you," Frank insisted.

"Didn't know you were my keeper," I said half jokingly, but only half. Since my divorce I'd enjoyed being able to make all my own decisions without having to get anyone else's permission.

I could tell Frank understood, as always. That was what I loved about him; he was so intuitive. "Sorry. But I would feel much better if you'd *let* me go with you." He said it with a smile as if asking for forgiveness.

"Okay," I said. "I guess four eyes are better than two. Let's do it tomorrow."

"Do you think you'll feel up to it?"

"I'm not going to be turning handsprings, just looking through drawers. I'm sure I can handle it. Another thing, we've never found out anything about Lana's boyfriend."

"Right. What was his name?"

"Herman James. Though we agreed nobody would call him Herman. It's three o'clock so the motorcycle shops will still be open. Why don't we call around and see if we can find him at one of them?"

"Sounds like a plan."

Frank and I took turns going through the list in the yellow pages. We were both surprised at how many shops there were in the area. And with the high cost of gas, we knew that they would be thriving with more people than ever opting for two-wheeled transportation these days.

When I called shop number eleven, Cruisin' Cycles, I finally tracked him down. "Does a Herman James work for you?" I asked.

"You mean Ham James?" the young voice asked. I had visions of a huge mountain of a man shaped like a whole ham, narrow at the top and wide through the middle.

"Yes, that's probably him. Is he there today?" Not that it made a difference because I wasn't going to question him over the phone. And I didn't feel like going anywhere at the moment.

"Nah. He's off till Monday."

Frank and I decided to go to the shop on Monday, two days from now, and see what we could learn about Ham James. I personally wasn't looking forward to it. I knew that Donna didn't approve of her daughter's boyfriend, so I wondered what kind of a guy we would encounter. And I was curious why Lana had to ask her dad for money. Ham should make decent wages fixing motorcycles, though I had no idea what the going rate might be for mechanics. It wasn't as though they paid high rent since he owned that run-down trailer. Where did their money go? And had they, or maybe just Ham, believed that Lana might inherit from her father?

SUNDAY MORNING the three of us set out to go through Fulton's house. Although Frank at first balked at having Nina accompany us, she convinced him to change his mind.

"Tommi's in worse shape than I am. I'm just fine. And I'll be bored out of my mind if you don't let me come." I had visions of her whining to get her way with her father when she was a kid. I'll bet he indulged her a lot.

Luckily I'd stuck the key in my jean's pocket when I'd gone in his place on Friday.

There was no way we all could sneak into Fulton's condo without anyone seeing us, so we went in bold as brass. And we shut and locked the door behind us though I couldn't imagine anyone trying to overpower all three of us.

Apparently someone from the police department had disposed of the dead rat—they probably couldn't tolerate the smell either—but we'd brought some Oust that managed to neutralize the residual smell.

We agreed to divvy up the rooms in our search. Frank took the kitchen, Nina the living room, and I went to the master bedroom upstairs.

I looked in the adjoining bathroom first. Sure enough, as Lana had told me, a woman's robe was hanging on the back of the door, a silk-like, polyester, wrap robe with purple blossoms. I looked at the label, and it was made by a manufacturer that was sold in every department store and discount store around. No help there. In the medicine cabinet I found some overnight moisturizer, which I assumed belonged to a woman unless Fulton was into male cosmetics that I understood some of the young, urban males now embrace. There was also some hair spray and women's deodorant, neither of which could I imagine Fulton using.

The other interesting thing I found was a bottle of Viagra. That spoke for itself.

The unmade bed didn't surprise me as I imagined most bachelors couldn't be bothered. But maybe I was being sexist.

I went through the dresser drawers, nightstand, and bookcase but couldn't find anything that screamed *I am a clue!* I guess I wanted something to jump out and bite me on the nose.

In the second bedroom I found two long folding tables laden with bolts of cloth. So this was where he stored his merchandise that he sold at reenactments. Looking closely, I saw that the ends of the cardboard forms that the yard goods were wrapped around had been altered. Sticky labels had been cut to fit exactly over the end. These held a description of the material: one-hundred percent wool, the price per yard, and Made in the Netherlands. I noticed I could carefully peel away the sticker to reveal the original information underneath: 50% wool, 30% polyester, 20% recycled materials, Made in China. The price was less than a third of that on the sticker. Fulton had probably paid even less than that at the wholesale price. He'd been making quite a killing. I wondered what had become of all the material he'd been selling at the Guilford Courthouse reenactment. Probably the police impounded it. I was looking at his extra stock.

An additional costume to the one he was wearing when he was killed hung in the closet, one that appeared to be lighter weight for summer use. On the closet shelf under a bunch of blankets and pillows was a ledger. I decided to show it to Frank and Nina. Since I'm not all that great with accounting, I figured they could make more sense out of it than I could.

When I went back downstairs, Nina had already completed her search, and Frank was working on the last cupboard.

"Find anything?" I asked.

"Nothing," Nina said, "other than a whole lot of bits of food and dust puppies. I'm surprised there aren't more mice running around."

"There might have been," I said, "but the smell of their dead buddy sent them fleeing. If they're that smart."

"I did come up with a phone bill," Frank said. "Unfortunately it's not from ACS so I can't check it out. But if he's making calls related to his scams, he'd probably use a cell phone. Too hard to trace those."

I told them of my discoveries in the bathroom and guest bedroom. "Best of all," I said, "I found his ledger. Maybe this will help."

"Let's have a look at it," Frank said taking it from me. We sat around the kitchen table as he scrutinized the book. I knew he'd had accounting in college so I hoped he could make heads or tails of it. He studied it at some length while Nina and I inspected our nails (mine were in terrible shape) and fidgeted. Finally he said, "It looks as though Fulton was not alone in his scam."

"Really?" I said. "Who else was involved?"

"Does the name Steve Leonard mean anything to you?"

"Steve Leonard. Steve Leonard," I mumbled to myself. "Oh, yes. I remember. He was the sutler in another tent selling costumes and weapons. Garland introduced me to him."

"Well, Fulton was paying money to Steve. And Steve was paying money to Fulton. I would say they'd conspired to share the spoils of their entrepreneurship. We don't know if Steve was cheating people as well, but I'd have to assume so."

"Oh, my God," I said. "This is really going to upset the people involved in the reenactment. I'm sure this kind of thing is a rare occurrence, but it's still going to be hard to take."

"Since Steve was making money from Fulton, he certainly wouldn't be his murderer," Nina said.

"No I wouldn't think so," I agreed. "Not that I ever considered him. It just adds another dimension to this mystery."

SEVENTEEN

JUST BEFORE WE LEFT I remembered that I was ostensibly there to make a list for a possible yard sale to give to Rhonda, so the three of us hurriedly went through the house debating the value of various pieces of furniture. Nina usually came in high, Frank low, so I chose a figure somewhere in the middle.

Instead of dropping it off at Rhonda's house, my notes were so messy and disorganized, I decided to write it up on Nina's computer and print it out. Then I could take it by Rhonda's when I went home.

None of us felt like going to a restaurant in our grungy work clothes, so we picked up Chinese take-out and ate at Nina's house. She and I felt like a nap while Frank read the newspaper. I was awake within the hour and typing up the list for Rhonda.

Once I printed it out I told Frank I wanted to go home. Even though he'd assured me he'd fed and scooped Tee when he picked up my clothes, I felt bad about leaving him alone for so long.

"I gave him enough food to last several days," he protested.

"You don't know Tee. He probably ate most of it

in one fell swoop and then barfed it up again. If it sits for very long I'll never get the stain out of my carpet."

That argument did the trick, and he agreed to drive me to my condo.

Nina was up by then, and I hugged her and thanked her for her hospitality. "We need to get together more often. And let me know when your treatments start."

She assured me she would.

I asked Frank to swing by Rhonda's house on the way home. "I want to give her this list," I said. "Then I can forget about that project until after the next board meeting. They'll have to approve the yard sale and set a date for it. Maybe I can even convince some other un-suspecting soul to head it up so I won't have to do it."

When I rang her bell I got no answer so I put the list, which I'd stuck in an envelope along with the key to Fulton's house, into her mailbox. I'd leave a message on her phone alerting her to it.

Tee greeted me at my door with a dubious stare to let me know I shouldn't have left him alone for so long. As always he wasn't sure whether he was thrilled to see me or mad enough to ignore me for a while. At first glance, at least, it looked as though he'd managed to keep his food down.

Frank insisted on coming into my house and searching it from top to bottom before he left.

"Come on, Frank," I said. "There aren't any boogey-men in here."

"With your track record, I'm never sure. Please keep your door locked at all times, will you?"

"Of course I will. I was already doing that."

He hesitated a moment before putting his arms around me and pulling me into a hug. "You gave me a real scare, Tommi. You may not realize how much you mean to me. I don't want anything to happen to you."

I cared a lot for him too, but I still wasn't sure whether he thought of me strictly as a good friend or as something more than that. So I said nothing but hugged him back.

He kissed the top of my head, then let me go and said, "Are we going to go talk to Ham James tomorrow?"

Well, I guess that was the answer. I was his friend. Period. *Bummer.* "Sure," I said brightly. "What time?"

I WOKE UP LATER than usual Monday morning feeling sluggish. Friday's incident had taken more out of me than I had realized. But it was impossible to stay in bed too long as Tee wouldn't let me. His desire for more food had overcome his displeasure that I'd left him alone. Cats are so egocentric.

It had been over a week since I'd talked to my boss, Logan Stahl. I gave him a call as soon as the office opened.

"Hi, it's Tommi," I said. "I hope you're managing okay without me."

"Of course," he said. "Lucy and I are doing just fine." Since Lucy had retired and was living on a fixed income, I knew the extra money was a big help to her so I didn't feel too guilty.

"She's made me two batches of brownies already," he said. I knew that made up for her lack of computer skills.

"I'm going to need more time off," I said. "I hope that's okay."

"As long as Lucy keeps feeding me, we'll carry on. Just don't let it stretch into months."

"Heavens no. If we can't get it wrapped up in another week or two, I'll tell Bernard he'll have to replace me."

Frank was coming at nine to take me to Cruisin' Cycles. While I was still in the hospital he'd picked up my Fit at the police impound lot and taken it to a body shop to have the right front panel repaired, and I wouldn't get it for a couple of days. It meant he'd had to take cabs to the lot and then from the repair shop back to the hospital parking deck where he'd left his car, so he'd really gone to a lot of trouble.

Since my purse had been stolen, I dug out another one from my closet and filled it with the usual stuff: lipstick, comb, Kleenex and so on. I'd have to go by the bank sometime and get some walking-around money, and I'd need a new billfold. What a pain in the neck it is when you lose something so essential to your daily life. I hoped that I'd soon get replacements for all the cards that had been stolen.

I had three cups of coffee; it seemed as if I added an extra one each day, and I'd soon be knocking off the whole pot. I'd be totally wired then. My customary cereal and banana sure beat the cold hospital eggs. I'd only begun to read the News and Record, normally a part of my morning ritual, when Frank rang the doorbell.

"Ready?" he asked. He looked considerably brighter and more cheerful than I felt.

CRUISIN' CYCLES WAS ON East Bessemer east of Summit Avenue. It was a one-story brick building about as non-descript as it could get. Rows of motorcycles were lined up in front, a variety of makes and models, old and new. Some looked very utilitarian while others had been fancied up till they looked like rolling art forms. Some of the large European-style motor scooters that were gaining popularity stood prominently in the front row.

We found a place to park at one side of the lot, and went into the showroom which displayed three of the biggest and fanciest models of cycles. I recognized the Gold Wing which is the size of a small car, or these days even bigger than some I suspected, but otherwise I knew nothing about motorcycles. I just knew I'd be too chicken to ride on one. I wondered if Frank ever had.

A burly guy dressed in a tee shirt with a Honda logo asked if he could help us.

"We're looking for Ham James," I said.

He jerked a thumb toward a door at the rear of the shop. "In there," he said, losing interest now that he knew we weren't there to buy a bike.

In the back room a small, skinny guy was working on the motor of an old cycle. Tools were scattered around him on the floor as were small unidentifiable parts. A couple of other motorcycles looking road-worn were parked at one side. So this was Ham. His name couldn't have been more misleading. He re-minded me a lot of Sonny Bono with a straggly ginger-colored mustache and thinning hair that was long enough to tie back in a ratty-looking ponytail. He certainly didn't appear very intimidating. But I knew that could be misleading because little guys sometimes can have quite a chip on their shoulders.

"Ham James?" Frank asked.

He'd been so absorbed in his work, he looked up surprised we were there.

"Yeah?" He looked from Frank to me and back to Frank again. I'm sure we didn't look like we were there on motorcycle business.

"I'm Frank and this is Tommi. Could we talk to you for a minute?"

Ham frowned. "I'm way behind here, man. Whadya want to talk about?"

I realized it would be awkward to interrogate him here. "Do you get a break any time soon? We could take you out for a cup of coffee and some sausage biscuits," I said. There was a Biscuitville restaurant a few doors down.

"I dunno." He fiddled with a small wrench.

"There'd be a fifty in it for you," Frank said. I was surprised. We'd never offered a bribe to anyone before, but perhaps in this case it was essential.

Ham looked at Frank for a minute as if trying to

size him up. "Yeah, guess I could take it a little early. Thirty minutes. That's all I can give ya."

We waited while Ham went into a bathroom to get the grease off his hands. He spoke quietly to the salesman out front, and the three of us walked down to the restaurant, the quintessential southern biscuit-and-gravy fast food emporium.

I got another cup of coffee which I knew would send me over the moon while the men got sweet tea and steak biscuits. We settled at a table by a window.

Ham took a swig of tea and bite of biscuit. Once his mouth cleared he said, "Okay. Whadya guys want?"

"Did you ever meet Lana's dad?" I asked.

He looked surprised. "How the hell d'you know Lana?"

"I live near where her dad lived. I've talked to her mom. I've talked to Lana as well."

"She tell you where I work?"

"She wouldn't even give me your name. But I have ways to find out," I said, trying to sound mysterious.

He narrowed his eyes suspiciously. "You with the cops or somethin'?"

"Nope. I'm doing this on my own."

"What the hell for?" Ham had a very limited vocabulary.

"Because a friend of mine was arrested for his murder. And I'm sure he didn't do it."

Ham stood up in alarm. "Hey, lady. You tryin' to

say I did?" A couple of customers two tables away gaped at us.

"No, of course not," I lied, waving him to sit down. "I just hoped maybe you could tell us something about Fulton that would help us."

He shook his head. "Dint hardly know the guy."

"You say 'hardly'" Frank said. "Had you met him?"

"Once or twice."

"And what did you think of him?" Frank asked.

Ham just shrugged his shoulders and kept on eating.

We had no idea in advance what we were going to ask him, but I suddenly had an inspired thought. "Are you sure you two weren't working some kind of con together?" I asked, trying to stare him down.

He put his biscuit down and tried, but failed, to look offended.

"Whadya mean?"

"You've been arrested for petty larceny." His eyes widened in surprise, and he tried to cover it up with a look of nonchalance, so I kept on going. "I've heard people say they think Fulton was stealing from his employer. Were you acting as his fence?"

Frank was sitting beside me, and he gave me a quick glance while suppressing a smile. I took his surreptitious elbow in my side to mean "Go, girl, go!"

Ham was flustered and it was obvious. "You gotta lot of nerve accusin' me of stuff. You ain't no cop."

"No, you're right. But it seems pretty logical to me. I'll bet Lana doesn't even know about it. Her mom told me she went to him for money and he turned her down. No wonder. You were making money off him. And, tell me if I'm wrong; you're not sharing any of it with Lana." I really thought Lana knew, but not because Ham told her. Why else was she looking at prices on eBay? She wanted to know how much Ham was holding out on her.

Ham looked scared now. I was pretty sure I had him figured right. He was a no-good, two-bit punk.

He wouldn't look me in the eye, but sat there playing with the top of one of his biscuit sandwiches, tearing it into tiny bits. Some tough guy.

"Look, Ham, I'd say that lets you off the hook as far as his murder is concerned. If you were making money off him, you wouldn't want him dead." I wasn't convinced of that. Something could have gone awry with their partnership. But I wanted him to think I'd eliminated him as a suspect. "So, we won't tell Lana what you were doing if you'd just answer some questions for us now." I guess I wasn't above blackmail myself, but I figured it was for a Higher Cause in this case.

Ham took a couple of deep breaths and put down the mutilated biscuit. "Okay," he said despondently.

"Let me ask you a question," Frank said. "I know Tommi said you wouldn't want Fulton killed, but where were you a week ago yesterday? That was Sunday of last week in the afternoon."

"Workin' on some bikes. You can ask Charlie. We got so much business these days we can't keep up with it. We got to work on Sundays now."

"Who's Charlie?"

"The salesman who's there today. He was there that day. Sold three bikes, I think."

"Okay, my turn," I said. "Do you know anything about a woman who was coming to his house only at night?"

"Well, yeah. He used to make jokes about her."

"Do you know her name?" Maybe at last we were getting somewhere.

"Naw. He called her 'rich bitch' sometimes. He never said so, but I think he was probably working a scam on her. That's the way he was."

"Any idea what that might be?" I asked.

"He dint tell me. But Ridenhour could dream up more ways to con people than anybody. He was a genius at it."

I believed him about Fulton's chicanery. But unless he had a hidden stash of money somewhere, he wasn't very successful. I didn't think he came even close to being a genius.

I asked Ham if he knew of any other specific scams.

"Not that he was runnin' now. But he'd told me of some he did out in Missouri."

We already knew about the embezzlement. And if there were others, they were probably too long ago and far away to be connected to his murder.

We'd wrung Ham dry of any information so we walked him back to the bike shop. Before we went inside, Frank pulled out his wallet and handed him a fifty. Ham stuck it in his pocket and hurried into the back room without another word. Before we left Frank asked Charlie to verify he'd been there on the fifteenth.

"Sure. Ham was here. It's been crazy 'round here since the price of gas went up."

When we got in the car, Frank said, "Do you think we should go see Bernard? We need to fill him in on what we found at Ridenhour's place and what Ham just told us."

"Good idea. I suspect he'll want us to check out Steve Leonard since he and Fulton certainly had something going on between them during reenactments. And we need to pass along the information about Ham being Fulton's fence. He might want to pass that on to the police."

"I dunno, Tommi," Frank said. "I feel like paying Ham for information sort of gave him immunity from that. If it were still going on it would be different, and I doubt he made much from it. It's kind of a quandary, isn't it?"

"Maybe so. His employer by now should be aware that Fulton was stealing from them. If so, the cops could probably track it down themselves."

We both sat in silence for a while worrying about the right thing to do.

Finally I spoke. "Let's explain all this to Bernard and let him make the decision. He's the legal eagle."

"But not the most compassionate guy around," said Frank.

I couldn't help but laugh. "You're talking about old Tender Heart?"

"That's the one."

We were almost downtown when another thought occurred to me. "Hey, Frank? Remember Ham said Fulton called his girlfriend 'rich bitch'? Then why would she be driving an old Ford? That's how two different people described the car."

"You're right, Tommi. That doesn't make much sense."

EIGHTEEN

BERNARD KEPT US WAITING only fifteen minutes, which surprised me since we didn't have an appointment. Usually he's so immersed in work, it takes him a while to disengage himself. He stood up and shook hands with Frank and nodded hello to me. We made ourselves comfortable in the two client chairs.

"I suppose you've heard the news," he said.

Frank and I looked at each other blankly. "We didn't have time to read the paper or watch TV this morning," I said. "What news?"

"Joe Kernodle is dead."

"What!" I yelped. "Where? How? Oh, my God!"

"His obituary was in the paper this morning. He died on Friday. Of course it didn't give a cause of death but said he died at Wesley Long Hospital. I know someone who knows someone who got me the information. It seems he fell down the stairs at his home and broke his neck."

"Oh, give me a break. I don't believe that for a minute," I huffed.

"Apparently the cops do. Investigated it, of course. Couldn't find anything to point elsewhere. Did you know he had a cat?"

"Joe Kernodle? He didn't seem the animal-lover type to me."

"Well, the neighbors confirm he's had a cat for several years. The theory is he tripped over the cat and fell."

How weird. I had a great uncle that happened to many years ago, but he was eighty-five and had poor eyesight. I supposed it could happen to a relatively young, healthy man, but it was just too much of a coincidence—again!

"I guess we need to look into that," I said.

Bernard nodded. "It could be just a fluke, but what's your take on it?"

"My take is the cops' decision is phony baloney. The strange thing is," I said, "my top suspect would be Fulton Ridenhour. Do you think he came back from the dead for revenge?"

"Not funny, Tommi," Frank said with a deadpan expression. "Let's have a little respect for the deceased."

"I do," I insisted. "I have the greatest respect for poor Sir Martingale."

Bernard shook his head. "You're incorrigible."

Between us Frank and I related our search of Fulton's house. "We found a ledger," I said, "that indicates that Fulton was working together with Steve

Leonard to fleece people at the reenactments. Apparently they were both overpricing their wares and sharing the profits."

"Do you know this guy?" Bernard asked.

"I met him briefly during the reenactment. Garland introduced me to him. His tent was near Fulton's," I said.

"So, conceivably, he could have killed Ridenhour."

"Perhaps a quarrel over how they split the money?" Frank suggested.

"Possibly." Bernard was tapping a pen repeatedly against the edge of the desk. It was probably to help him think, but it was driving me crazy.

Finally I said, "Enough with the drumming, Bernard. My head hurts."

He frowned. He didn't like me to remind him of his O.C. tendencies. "Sorry, didn't realize I was doing it. Anyway, the list of suspects continues to grow. What else have you learned?"

"We talked to the boyfriend of Fulton's daughter," Frank said. "He acted as a fence for stuff that Ridenhour stole from his place of work."

"Good Lord," Bernard said, "I don't know how he kept track of all the scams he had going."

I explained to Bernard that Frank had not only paid Ham for information, but had essentially blackmailed him into talking. "Since Fulton's obviously not stealing any more, I was hoping it wouldn't be necessary to alert the police to Ham's involvement. Can't we let that slide?"

Bernard reassured me. "I'm not required to report that as an officer of the court. Do you think there's any chance that this guy could have been Ridenhour's killer?"

"No," Frank said. "He was working at the motor-cycle shop at the time. The salesman verified that for us."

"Okay, let's concentrate on Steve Leonard, and see if you can find out anything about Joe Kernodle's death."

"Aye, aye, sir." I stood up and saluted.

When we got back to the car I used my cell phone to call the Merritts. I hadn't touched base with them since my stint in the hospital. I hoped Garland might be able to fill me in about Steve Leonard. The reen-actors were a tightly knit bunch.

Constance opened the door when I rang their bell.

She embraced me in a huge hug and said, "It's so good to see you, Tommi. We're hoping you can catch us up on things. We haven't heard a word from Bernard." She suddenly realized Frank was standing behind me. "Oh, hello," she said pulling away from me. "I'm Constance Merritt."

"Frank Poag."

I could see the confusion in Constance's eyes. "He's Bernard's cousin," I said. "He lives in Wiscon-sin, but he's moving back to Greensboro."

She smiled and shook his hand. "Welcome back."

Garland had just come down the stairs, and introductions were made and the men shook hands. "Come in and have a seat." He looked tired and worried. The strain of a possible murder trial had to be overwhelming. I wanted so much to lift the burden from both of them.

"I'm so sorry I haven't been able to keep you more up to date the past couple of days," I said. "I know it's got to be the worst thing you've ever been through. But a lot has happened since I talked to you last."

When I told them about Friday and described the mugging and stabbing I'd endured, they were horrified.

"Tommi!" Constance exclaimed. "I can't let you do this if you're at risk! I'd never forgive myself if anything else happened. Please, please stop your investigation."

"Connie is right," Garland added. "We can't let you continue."

I understood and appreciated their concern. But I couldn't stop. I felt that things would start to jell soon. I was sitting beside Frank on the sofa and I patted his arm. "I have a bodyguard now. I'll be perfectly safe." I turned and smiled at him and squeezed his arm a little because I knew what he was thinking: that he hadn't managed to keep me safe on Friday. But that was because he was at the hospital with Nina.

I'm sure he read my thoughts. "I'm not going to let her out of my sight when she's out of her house," he said. "My daughter is doing very well now, and she doesn't need me to be with her at this time." I'd told them about Nina's operation. "So Tommi may get sick and tired of having me around, but until she gets what she's after, I'm sticking with her like Velcro."

Constance sighed and shook her head. "Oh, Tommi, I never should have asked you in the first place."

"Once they arrested Garland, you couldn't have kept me away," I said. "So let me tell you what's happened since Friday."

I brought her up to date and told her about today's meeting with Bernard. "You heard about Joe Kernodle, I imagine."

"I was stunned," Constance said. "I suppose they'll figure out some way to implicate Garland in that."

"You don't need to worry," I assured her. "Bernard managed to find out what happened. Or what the police think happened. They're saying he tripped over his cat and fell down the stairs."

"Joe?" Garland asked, sounding amazed. "He had a cat?"

"Seems unlikely, doesn't it? I wonder what happened to the poor kitty. Do you think someone is taking care of it?" I asked.

"I don't know," Constance said. "I know Joe was divorced. I don't know if he had kids or not."

I turned to Frank. "We need to go to his neighbors.

Find out what happened to it. I wonder if somebody took it to the pound. If so, we need to rescue it."

"And do what with it?" Frank asked. He sounded a bit dubious about my concern.

"Do you think Nina would like a cat?"

"With all that expensive upholstery in her house? Can you imagine what the cat's claws would do to it?"

I'm sure they all thought I'd lost my mind. All these momentous matters to deal with and I go babbling on about a cat. But Fulton's dog had died, and I couldn't bear the thought of another animal being put to sleep. "I guess I could take it myself." I tried to imagine how Tee would react to that—Mr. Lord of the Universe.

Frank just shook his head. "We'll see what we can do."

I was anxious to change the subject before they decided to have me committed. "Garland, what can you tell me about Steve Leonard?"

"May I ask why?"

I told him about finding the ledger in Fulton's house that implicated him in a scam.

"That's very troubling. I've never heard of anything like that happening on the reenactment scene."

"They were just two bad eggs," I said. "Can't you report this somehow so it's handled quietly, and doesn't give a black eye to the groups? They don't deserve the bad publicity."

"Yes, I think so. It's mainly the reenactors who

were hurt because they make up most of the customers. So let's hope we don't have to compound the injury by having it go public."

"What do you know about Steve's background?" Frank asked.

"He moved here some years ago from out west somewhere. Not sure where. He works as a department manager at Walmart. Single, at least now. Never heard if he was ever married or not."

"When did he get involved in reenactments?"

Garland thought about it for a while. "Now that you mention it, I believe he and Fulton started about the same time. That would be four or five years ago. If memory serves me, they acted as if they didn't know each other at first, like they'd just met."

"So they could have planned in advance what they were going to do, and then pretended to be strangers," I said. "That way no one would have suspected them of doing anything illegal."

I told Garland and Constance how Fulton had re-labeled his yard goods to indicate it was pure wool when it wasn't.

"Thank God I already had my uniform made before he came," Garland said. "But there are going to be some very upset people. It's a huge amount of work to put one of those outfits together. Then to find out that it's not the material they thought it was is going to make them very angry."

"But what about Steve?" I asked. "He sells firearms

and finished clothing. Is it possible to get cheap knockoffs of those?"

"Oh, I'm sure it is. A Brown Bess can sell for up to eleven hundred dollars. Probably could get them made in China or somewhere for a whole lot less."

"What's a Brown Bess?" I asked.

"The nickname for one of the most famous muskets of the times. It was developed in Britain and was used as the standard gun of their land forces from 1722 until the eighteen thirties. The Americans used them as well."

Garland never ceased to amaze me with his knowledge of the era.

"And ladies' dresses can sell up to four or five hundred dollars for a ball gown," he continued. "You know that he could probably get cheap imitations from the Far East."

"It's like those guys on New York sidewalks selling designer knockoff purses and shoes," Constance said.

"Rolex watches," chimed in Frank.

"Somehow I never imagined that kind of chicanery would come to reenactments," Garland said.

"Hopefully this is a first," I said, as if that would give him comfort. "And the last. Anyway, I'd like to find out more about him. Do you know where he lives? Maybe I can make up an excuse to talk to him."

"Somewhere in Green Valley I think, on Cornwallis."

How ironic that Steve lived on a street named after the British general who fought in the battle of Guilford Courthouse.

"Anything else?"

"Not that comes to mind."

We said goodbye to the Merritts, and because we were so close to my house, I asked Frank to come there for lunch. I had some luncheon meat and cheese in the fridge that I was afraid would go bad if I didn't use it up soon. And it would give us a chance to relax a bit. We couldn't very well interview Steve at work at Walmart so that would have to wait for evening. I suggested that after lunch we talk to Joe Kernodle's neighbors and see if they had any ideas about his "accident." I honestly doubted if we could find out much about his death, but I hoped to find out where his cat was.

When I opened my front door, I noticed the smell immediately. It was the strong odor of leaking gas.

"Don't go in there!" Frank shouted. "I'm calling 9-1-1!" And he turned on his heel to race to his car for his cell phone.

But all I could think of was Tee. I took a deep gulp of fresh air, held my breath and dashed inside. Tee was crumpled lifelessly on the living room floor. Scooping him up, I raced back outside. I couldn't tell if he was dead or unconscious. All I could do was sit on the curb cradling him in my arms, cooing, "Wake up, Tee, wake up."

Once Frank had called the fire department, he began pounding on the doors on either side of me to alert the residents. When I realized what he was doing I called to him, "They'll all be at work, Frank."

Running back to me, he helped me to my feet still holding Tee, and guided me across the street. "If it blows, Tommi, you don't want to be close."

The fire trucks were there in a matter of minutes. Within a few more minutes, they'd shut off the gas, opened all the windows wide, and had placed giant floor fans at the doors to blow out the fumes.

One of the men held an oxygen mask over Tee's face. Within a short while he began to stir, opened his eyes, and gave a weak "meeoww." Tears were streaming down my face when they handed him back to me.

"What happened in there?" Frank asked the fireman who seemed to be in charge.

"All the burners on the stove were wide open, but there was no flame. Any kind of spark, and the place would have blown up. Do you two know how that happened?"

"No," I said. "I've been gone all morning. We could smell it the minute I opened the door."

His glance fell on Tee. "Do you think your cat could have done that somehow?"

"No way. Even if he had managed to turn on a burner, he's scared to death of fire. He couldn't have put the flames out."

"Does anyone else have a key to your house?"

"I gave one to Mr. Poag here. But he was with me. That's the only one."

"We'll have to get our investigators on it. We'll

stay here with the fans another thirty minutes or so, and then you can go in your house safely."

And so we waited in the car with Tee on my lap. I was still trembling from the thought of not only coming close to losing my house, but the shock of thinking that Tee was dead.

NINETEEN

By the time we were able to go back in my house, we'd both lost our appetites. We sat slumped on the sofa, trying to come to terms with what had just happened.

"So now you see why I said I was sticking by your side no matter what," Frank said.

"So you can get killed too?"

"I'm not going to let that happen. Though if I didn't know you better and realize I couldn't talk you out of continuing this, I'd be on the Merritts' side."

"And let Garland go to jail for something he didn't do." It was a statement, not a question. I was trying to shame Frank into seeing my point of view.

"Tommi, you've got to realize that you can't always right every wrong."

"I'm not trying to right *every* wrong. I just won't let my friends or loved ones be falsely accused."

Frank sighed deeply. "Okay, this conversation is getting us nowhere. Let's try to think about how this happened today."

"I'm wondering if I left my patio door unlocked. I let Tee out on the patio early this morning, and I always lock the door when he comes back in. But I had a lot on my mind." I walked to the back of the house to the small dining area to check the sliding door. "Oh, no," I said. "Of course it's unlocked now because the firemen had one of their fans in front of it. There's no way to check what I did when I let Tee in. I think I was on auto pilot at the time."

"There's no lock on the gate to your patio is there?"

"No, just a latch. Never thought I needed a lock."

"It might not be a bad idea. Though if anyone was determined to get in, they could always scale the fence."

"You're right, Frank. It would be pointless."

"Okay, then, where do we go from here?" Frank asked.

"Let's go talk to Joe Kernodle's neighbors."

More than anything I wanted to find out about his cat. If I could save it, it would be the one bright spot in an otherwise dismal week.

According to the phone book his condo was three blocks away. It looked as though his model was similar to mine: living/dining space, kitchen and laundry room downstairs, two bedrooms and a bath up. There were three or four different two-story models and a single-story model at the ends of each row in our development.

No one answered the door at the house to the right of Joe's. But a young man in his twenties was at home on the other side. He had a pleasant face framed by shoulder-length hair, and wore a UNCG tee shirt with his jeans.

I introduced myself and Frank. "I knew Joe

Kernodle," I said. "We were on the homeowners' board together. I wondered if we could talk to you for a minute."

"Sure," he said inviting us in. "I work second shift, so I don't have to leave just yet. By the way, I'm Ken Parks."

It looked as though Ken had moved straight from a college dorm to his condo. The living room was sparsely furnished with a well-worn canvas butterfly chair in orange and a green futon equally well used. Frank and I sat on it.

"I'd heard that Joe tripped over his cat and fell down the stairs," I began.

Ken nodded. "That's the story."

"The story?" I asked. "Do you mean made-up story, or do you believe it really happened?"

"I don't know. I'd been in Joe's house several times, and I never saw his cat. It was one of the fraidy-cat types that spend most of the time under the bed."

"But you're sure he had one."

"Oh, God, yes. You could smell it the minute he opened the door. I don't think he cleaned the litter box very often."

"Do you think he abused it?"

"No, he seemed to think it was pretty cool, said he'd rescued it off the street. That was probably why it hid all the time. It was just that Joe was one lousy house-keeper."

"What happened to it?"

"The neighbors on the other side of Joe offered to

take it temporarily. I think they ended up taking it to the pound though. They have a big dog that hates cats. I'm allergic to them, so I couldn't help."

"Who found Joe's body?" Frank asked. I knew he was trying to steer me away from what he thought of as my compulsive interest in the kitty.

"What I heard was that Joe didn't show up at work and didn't call in on Friday. He never missed a day, so his boss asked the police to check on him. And, voila, there he was at the bottom of the stairs with a broken neck."

"Do you know why the cops thought he tripped on the cat?" Frank asked. "How would you know unless you saw it happen?" That had occurred to me too. I thought it was a stretch to blame it on the poor animal.

"They found the cat with a broken paw at the bottom of the stairs next to Joe's body. They think Joe accidentally stepped on its paw and that sent them both tumbling down the steps. You know cats—they manage to land on four feet…or in this case three, I guess."

Now I knew I had to find that kitty. No one was going to adopt one that was injured. Except me.

We thanked Ken and got up to leave. On the way out the door I thought to ask him, "What was the cat's name and what did he look like?"

"It's a she. Her name is Stacy. But as I said I never saw her."

Back in the car, I told Frank I wanted to go to the animal shelter. "I've got to have Stacy," I said.

"Don't you have enough on your mind already?" he asked. His patience was wearing a little thin.

"Well, if I can bring her home that would be one less thing. Otherwise, I'll keep fretting about her."

"Okay. You win," Frank said. He still might have thought I'd gone round the bend, but he respected my feelings. So we headed toward West Wendover Avenue.

TWO HOURS LATER we were on our way back to my house with a very frightened Stacy in an animal carrier. We'd stopped on the way to the shelter to buy a second litter box and the carrier, and she was cowering in it now. She was a lovely cat, white with dark gray splotches, and her broken paw was in a splint. I felt relieved and elated that we'd been able to find her.

I had no idea what kind of a reception she'd get from Tee.

He'd lorded it over the house for so long, I was sure he wouldn't like the idea of having to share my affection. Frank carried her into the house and set the carrier on the living room floor. Tee, still a little woozy, sniffed all around it. Surprisingly he seemed pretty disinterested; mainly, I think, because he still wasn't fully recovered. I carried Stacy to the spare bedroom, let her out and closed the door. By the time I'd brought her food and drink and a litter box, she'd disappeared under the bed. This was going to take a lot of patience. But I knew I had to give both of them time to get used to the idea they were going to share the same space.

When I got back downstairs, Frank declared he was starved, and I realized I was hungry too. We hadn't had a bite since breakfast.

I talked him into going to Panera's on Lawndale where I could get a filling bowl of chicken noodle soup along with a salad. Frank ordered their French onion soup and a smokehouse turkey hot Panini.

"How are we going to approach Steve Leonard?" he asked when we got to a booth.

"I don't think we want him to know we saw the ledger. We could just say we're talking to a number of people involved in the reenactment."

"That should work."

It was after seven-thirty when we'd finished eating, and we hoped to find Steve at home. I'd nixed the idea of calling ahead. "I don't want him to give us an excuse why we can't come." I said.

Steve lived in an attractive brick ranch house not far from Benjamin Parkway. A black Lexus was in the driveway so I felt sure he was home.

"He drives a Lexus? On a Walmart paycheck? I doubt it," Frank said.

"Don't forget he has 'outside income' from his scams."

"My guess is that he's been spending his, while Fulton was stashing his away."

When we rang the doorbell, the big burly man I remembered from the reenactment answered the door. His bushy beard had been recently trimmed and his hair was a bit shorter. I suspected he'd let it grow out for the battle reenactment. This time he was wearing a tight tee shirt that showed off his impressive muscular physique. I wouldn't want to tangle with this guy. He made Frank look frail by comparison.

Even after I introduced myself and Frank and told him I'd met him at his tent at the encampment, it was obvious he didn't remember me. But there was no particular reason he should.

"May we talk to you for a minute?" I asked.

"What about?" He clearly was annoyed that we were bothering him.

"I'm a friend of Garland Merritt who introduced me to you at the battle. I'm working with Garland's attorney. I'm sure you know that he was arrested for the murder of Fulton Ridenhour."

"Yeah, I heard that. That was pretty shocking."

"Well, since you and Fulton were both sutlers, I thought maybe you might have seen or heard something that could help in his case."

"Sorry. Didn't see a thing. There was another tent between us, and I had no idea anything happened till that woman started screaming."

"Could we come in and talk about it some more?" Frank asked. "Maybe some little thing happened you've forgotten that might help us. If we go over the events of the day, it might come back to you."

"No, I don't think so. I can't be any help. And I'm busy right now." He stepped back and closed the door.

That left Frank and I looking at each other in amazement.

"Well," I said, "I guess we're not welcome here."

Frank shrugged and signaled me to return to the car. Once inside he said, "We can't be too surprised. Steve has a lot to hide. And we shouldn't have expected him to cooperate. We've been lucky up to now that everyone else has talked, although not always willingly."

"You're right, Frank. We have no authority. We're not like the cops, so it's a wonder we've been as successful as we have."

"It's been a long day. Tommi. I think we need to get some rest, and then tomorrow we can figure out what to do next."

He dropped me off at my house, checked it out thoroughly, and said he'd see me in the morning. After a hug and a quick kiss, more brotherly than I liked, he left.

So, where did we stand? I wish to heck I knew. As far as the case or our personal relationship was concerned, I was not a lot further ahead than I'd been at the beginning.

TWENTY

BERNARD CALLED ME first thing in the morning. I'd fed both cats, Stacy in the bedroom, although she was still under the bed, and Tee downstairs. He was acting a little needy because of yesterday's events.

"I found out something interesting," Bernard said. "The person who notified the local bar that Ridenhour had cheated on the exam in Missouri was Steve Leonard."

"Holy cow!" I said. "They were supposed to be buddies. I doubt very much that Fulton knew about that, because according to his ledger they were working together as recently as this month."

"Have you talked to him?"

"Frank and I tried to last night, but he claimed he knew nothing. Wouldn't even let us in the house."

"Not too surprising."

I told Bernard about talking to Joe Kernodle's neighbor. "I tracked down the cat that caused the accident. It had been taken to the animal shelter, so I adopted it."

"Thank God Pam doesn't like cats," he said. He'd never let me have a pet when I'd been married to him. Being able to have Tee had done a lot to heal me after our divorce. Why did I ever marry a man who didn't like animals? That should have been a clue.

"So where do you go from here?" he asked.

"I honestly don't know. I'll talk it over with Frank when he gets here."

Frank called me shortly after I hung up. "Nina has a doctor's appointment this morning that I'd forgotten about. I feel that I should go with her to give her moral support."

"I understand, Frank. That's most important. I can hang out this morning and do a little housework. Lord knows I need to."

"I contacted the body shop and your car is ready. I made arrangements for them to deliver it to you this morning. So you'll need to take the driver back to the shop. But, please, don't go anywhere else till I can be with you."

What a worry wart. "It'll be good to get my car back. Thanks, Frank." I purposely didn't agree to stay home, but I did intend to be very, very careful.

The guy from the shop brought my car about forty-five minutes later, and my little Fit looked good as new. Of course I never saw it when it was damaged. I took him back to the shop off of Spring Garden Street, and instead of going directly home, I decided to go visit Shirley Hayes and see how she was doing.

She gave me a hug when she opened the door and welcomed me inside. "As you can see," she said, "I haven't done much more unpacking. Just enough to get by for the month. But come sit down."

We sat on either end of her yellow-flowered sofa. The boxes were still stacked against the wall but the kitchen was cleared enough that it would be possible to fix a meal.

"I was just wondering how things were going," I said.

"So much better. You can't imagine what a burden you and Frank lifted off our shoulders. Bob's so thankful to you guys. He's planning a little party for you when we get back into our home."

"That's not necessary," I said. "Knowing we could help you is all the thanks we need."

She waved me off. I had a hunch they'd do it no matter how much I protested.

"Have you made any progress finding out who killed Fulton?" she asked.

"We're getting closer, but we're not quite there yet. I was wondering if you could give me any better description of the car you saw in front of his house now that you've had some time to think about it."

"Umm, I did remember something, but I didn't think it was important enough to call you."

"What was that?"

"I noticed that the hubcaps on the driver's side didn't match. There was just enough streetlight to see that the front one had more spokes than the back."

"That could be really helpful, Shirley," I said, though I couldn't imagine looking at every old Ford in town to check their wheels, if it was a Ford in the first place. She hadn't been certain about that. I stood up to leave. "We'll stay in touch. And I'm looking forward to having you back in the neighborhood."

I decided to go home and wait for Frank. He said he could probably get there after lunch if they weren't held up at the doctor's office.

Just as I turned off Lawndale onto Cottage Place, I saw a Lexus coming toward me that looked very much like the one that had been in Steve's driveway the night before. Surely he would be at work at Walmart, I thought. As the car neared, I saw it was a woman driving, and as it passed me, I realized it was Rhonda. What on earth? I knew there had to be a number of black Lexuses in town, but still...

She recognized me as we passed and gave a little wave. I waved back.

A block away I turned around and headed out to Walmart. I didn't expect to see the Lexus there, but I had decided to look for something else.

One of the stores is not far from my home. I took a right turn on Lawndale Drive and a left on Cotswald Terrace and a within a couple of blocks came to one of the smaller Walmarts in town. I didn't know if it was the one where Steve worked, but I had to start somewhere. I began to drive up and down the rows of cars in the parking lot looking for an older dark Ford with mismatched hubcaps. I'd almost given up hope when I got to the far side of the lot next to a wooded ravine. I saw an old navy blue Escort at the end of the row. I parked a few spaces away and got out to look at the wheels. Sure enough, the wheels on the driver's side didn't match.

I locked my car, hurried into the store and up to the Customer Service desk.

Two customers were ahead of me. I fidgeted nervously until finally I reached the counter.

"Say," I told the clerk, "I noticed a navy blue Escort out in the parking lot had a flat tire." I gave her the license number I had written down. "Maybe you should announce it over the loudspeaker so the driver can get it fixed. I'd hate for them to be surprised when they get there with a cart full of purchases."

"Thank you," she said. "I'll announce it right away."

I scurried out of the store and back to my car and scrunched down in the driver's seat to watch my rearview mirror.

Within five minutes I saw Steve Leonard pass by. He was staring straight ahead muttering to himself, probably profanities, and never glanced my way. Once he passed, I craned my neck and saw him go to the Escort and kick the tires. Of course they were all fine. I lay down on the seat so he couldn't see me as he stomped back to the store.

So! Steve's car had probably been in his garage the night before. Was it Rhonda's car in the driveway? If so, no wonder he wouldn't let us in the house.

Once I was sure that Steve was inside I drove back home. Now I was anxious to bounce this latest news off Frank.

FRANK SHOWED UP a little after two. He said that the doctor's appointment went well and Nina would begin her radiation therapy treatment in another week.

"Of course she's nervous about it," He said. "But the doctor told her that the newer treatments were less likely to have such bad side effects. So she's trying very hard to be upbeat about it."

"I've had some friends who've gotten through it very well. Wouldn't it be easier for her to stay with me while she's doing this so she doesn't have so far to drive back and forth?"

"That's kind of you, Tommi. I'll ask her. I don't have much more vacation time coming to me so I'm going to have to go back to work pretty soon, and that would be helpful. I see you got your car back. Did they do a good job?"

"Looks good as new."

"So what have you been up to today?"

I knew this question was coming. I had to share what I found out with him, but I knew he wasn't going to be pleased that I'd done it on my own. "I drove over to see Shirley Hayes. Just wanted to make sure she was getting along all right."

Frank frowned. "I thought you were going to wait for me before you did anything."

"Come on, Frank. Going to see Shirley wasn't dangerous. Please don't become controlling. That's too much like Bernard used to be."

He sighed. "You've got me between a rock and a hard place, Tommi. I know I'm not your keeper. But if anything happened to you I'd…" He seemed unable to finish the sentence. He took my hand and squeezed it. "Just please, please be careful."

I felt contrite—at least a little. "I will, cross my heart. Now, sit down and relax and get a grip because I have something else to tell you."

He flashed me an accusing look, but did as I asked. He took two deep breaths, rubbed his temples, said a silent mantra of some kind and said, "Okay. Shoot."

I told him about Shirley remembering the different hubcaps on the car parked in front of Fulton's. Before he could comment, I continued on about passing Rhonda in a black Lexus, going to Walmart, and finding Steve's car.

By the time I was done, Frank's eyes were wide and his mouth was agape. "So, what you're saying is it looks like Rhonda and Steve know each other."

"Intriguing, isn't it?"

"I'd say a better word is suspicious."

"I've been thinking about it since this morning. If Rhonda was at Steve's house and Steve was at Fulton's house, I would guess something was going on between the three of them. And I would guess it wasn't on the up and up."

- "Why weren't they all meeting together then?"

"They could have been. Rhonda's within walking distance of Fulton's. She could walk over there under cover of darkness and no one would notice. Everyone is glued to their television set or in bed late at night." I said. "Besides, Ham James had told us Fulton made jokes about a 'rich bitch,' and we did find a robe and cosmetics at his house."

Frank thought about this for a while. "I wonder what they could have been doing. Remember, Rhonda's name wasn't in that ledger."

"That's true. But Fulton certainly wasn't pulling just one scam. He was doing many."

"Okay, but you told me Rhonda called a special meeting to deal with the suit Fulton had filed over the death of his dog. Wouldn't she be a party to that if they were working together? Why would she send Constance, Joe, and you to try to talk him out of it?"

He made a good point. "That's a tough question, Frank. But you know, I wonder if she thought she was sending the three most inept members of the board to deal with him. I was brand new, and she probably considered Constance nothing but a troublemaker. She figured we'd never be able to stand up against Fulton. Rhonda had to act like she was doing something about it."

"And Joe?"

"Everyone thought Joe was a blowhard. I'm sure she never dreamed he would have a friend who was a PI and could dig up dirt about Fulton."

We both sat in silence for a while trying to put this all together. There were a lot of loose ends to tie up if we were anywhere near the truth.

"Do you think one of them killed Fulton?" Frank asked.

"I do. Of course the hard thing to figure is why."

"Maybe they all planned to share the proceeds of the suit if he won it and were furious when he gave in to Joe."

"I would say their chances of winning the suit weren't all that good, and after splitting it three ways, it would only amount to about thirty-three thousand each less lawyer's fees. That doesn't seem like much to kill for," I said. Of course that sum would be a considerable windfall for me. "Anyway, that scam was dead in the water so why kill him?"

"Rage, pure and simple. Fulton caved and they were mad about it."

"Because they were out their share?" I couldn't imagine going to that extreme for any amount of money.

"Are you kidding?" Frank asked. "People kill for much, much less than that."

"I guess you're right. Though I heard that Rhonda had inherited money and that was why she didn't work. Why does she need more?"

"Tommi, Tommi, some people never have enough."

"So what we've got to do is find out if the three of them were really working together, what the motive for the murder was, and which one killed him."

"Don't forget Joe," Frank said.

"Oh, Lord, I almost did. That almost certainly is connected. Maybe if we could find out why he was killed, it might give us the other answers."

"That's the tricky part," Frank said. "But now that we've put this much together, I'm more worried about you than ever. Two attempts have been made on your life, and it almost has to be either Rhonda or Steve. They're both aware now that they were unsuccessful, so you can bet they'll try something else. I'm going to insist you let me stay with you. I don't even mind sharing the guest-room with Stacy. But I'm not going to leave you alone."

I'd been so absorbed in trying to solve the puzzle I hadn't even gotten to the place I could acknowledge that. But he was right. I shuddered a little. I think I'm pretty brave, but I'm not stupid. "Okay," I said meekly. "Now that you mention it, I'd place my bet on Rhonda. She gave me the key to Fulton's place. What do you want to bet she put the dead mouse in there knowing I'd have to leave the door open to get rid of the smell."

"What about here? Could she get in and turn on the gas jets?"

"I don't know. I'm still not sure I didn't leave the sliding glass door open."

"We've got to find a way we can wrap this up," Frank said. "What do you suggest?"

"I suggest we set a trap."

"I don't like the sound of that, Tommi. When you say trap, do you mean you are the bait?"

"What else can we do?"

"Anything but that."

We argued and argued, but he would have none of it, even though he'd said he wouldn't try to tell me what to do. Finally, just to change the subject I said,

"Why don't we talk to Ham James once more. He worked with Fulton. And he might not have told us everything. Let's pump him a little harder."

"Okay," Frank agreed. I'm sure he was glad to do anything that would take my attention away from setting a trap for the rats in which I was the hunk of cheese.

TWENTY-ONE

WE DROVE ACROSS TOWN to Bessemer Avenue and pulled into Cruisin' Cycles. Charlie the salesman started to approach us as we entered the showroom, but must have recognized us and stopped short. By nodding his head in that direction, he sent us to the back room.

Ham was again bent over a motorcycle engine, totally absorbed in it. He turned around when Frank cleared his throat.

"Oh, God, you again? I thought you was gonna leave me alone."

"We thought maybe you didn't tell us everything last time," Frank said. He stood over skinny Ham trying to look as intimidating as possible. It was so unlike the real Frank that it almost made me laugh.

"We think you were in it deeper with Fulton than you let on," Frank continued. "Or at least you know more about what he was doing than you said. We're getting very close to finding out who killed him. Do you want to go down with them?"

Ham's eyes were filled with fear. "I told you I was workin' here when it happened."

"Yes, but you know something about it, don't you?" I decided it was time to join in.

"Let's get outta here," Ham whined. "I don't want Charlie to hear what we're talkin' about."

"Okay," Frank said. "Might as well fill up that skinny belly of yours."

"Biscuitville ain't open," Ham said. "They close after lunch."

"There's a McDonald's up on Summit," I said.

So Ham told Charlie he was taking his afternoon break, and the three of us piled into Frank's car. Soon Charlie was eating a Big Mac, and Frank and I were drinking diet cokes.

"Okay, Ham, start talking," Frank said. "We don't want to have to tell Lana about you."

Ham gave him a dirty look. He must have been wondering how long we were going to hold this over his head.

"Ridenhour told me was teamed up with his rich bitch girl friend and a guy who worked at Walmart. They was runnin' bunches of scams together. Both guys was stealin' from work, and his girl friend was cookin' the books somewheres. I dunno where. He tole me he and the other guy were makin' bunches of dough when they do these Revolutionary War battles. They sold stuff for way more 'an it was worth. They prob'ly had other stuff goin' on too. But they was like a gang, share and share alike. All I did was fence some of the stuff they stole."

That's all? I thought. Poor boob. I'm afraid he was

going to get caught up in the middle of all this when it came crashing down. Even if we did say we'd try to keep his name out of it.

"Do you know if the three of them had a falling out?" I asked.

Ham twitched at the suggestion. He didn't want to look me in the eye. Finally he said, "I reckon so."

"Can you tell us what it was?" I felt like I was talking to a child. I wanted to snarl "Look at me!" But I didn't.

"Last time I saw Ridenhour he was mad as hell. Said the bitch had double-crossed him, caused him to lose a bunch of dough.

Said he was gonna get his revenge."

Wow! Now we were getting somewhere. "Did he say how he was going to do that?" Frank asked.

Ham shook his head no vigorously. He at least knew better than to put himself in the position of having prior knowledge of whatever Fulton intended to do.

But a thought occurred to me. "Did you decide to make a little money by warning his girlfriend of his intentions?"

"No! I tole you I dint know who she was!" But his eyes said something else. Ham James would make a terrible poker player.

"Come on, Ham," Frank coaxed. "You know, don't you?"

But Ham continued to protest his ignorance. No amount of coercion would get him to tell us. He was much more afraid of a living person than a dead one. And who wouldn't be?

HAM WAS SO GLAD to get out of our car and back to the safety of Cruisin' Cycles he never said goodbye and literally ran into the building.

"I'm going to Nina's house and pack a suitcase," Frank said. "You may have me as a guest for a while until this is all resolved."

"But Nina needs you."

"She's not going to start treatment for a few days, so she's fine by herself for now. In the meantime, I'm not going to let you be alone."

I couldn't argue with him. I wanted to tell him I wasn't at all afraid, but he would have known I was lying. And I was glad to have a chance to see Nina. I wanted to invite her to stay with me while she was undergoing radiation because it was closer to the hospital. If Frank was still in my guest room, she and I could share my queen-size bed. God, I hoped that we could wind this up before that happened.

Frank suggested we get take-out from Lucky 32 and take it with us. That sounded good to me. So we got grilled salmon salads and apple pie for all of us.

Nina was in great spirits, and we had a good chat while Frank packed. We steered clear of talking about anything negative, murders and treatment, and talked about frivolous things. It did both of us a world of good.

After we ate, we headed back to my house. Nina had given Frank her blessing about staying with me. She was as fearful as he was for my safety.

"ARE YOU SURE you don't mind sharing the room with Stacy?" I asked him.

"I doubt that she'll come out from under the bed," he said.

I knew that Tee was going to be frustrated because I usually kept my bedroom door open so he could come and go as he pleased. I'd have to shut him out for a while.

"If you don't mind, I'm exhausted," I said. "I'm going upstairs to read in bed."

"I'm pretty wound up myself. I'm going to watch TV for a while."

I wasn't as tired as I claimed, but I wanted some privacy. Frank would have a meltdown if he knew what I planned to do.

Once in my bedroom I called Rhonda. I thought it might help to prime the pump so to speak.

"Hi," I said. "It's Tommi. You know I found out something interesting I wanted to share with you. Did you know that Fulton Ridenhour not only was trying to put one over on the homeowners' association, but he and some other guy were pulling a scam during Revolutionary War reenactments? We found a ledger that showed what they were doing. I think they were involved in other things as well. I'm turning it all over to the police."

"How about that," Rhonda said innocently. "I always figured him for some kind of con man."

"Well, I'm sorry he's dead, but isn't it odd that Joe died too? After making sure that Fulton dropped his suit."

"Yes, that is quite a coincidence. I heard he tripped over his cat."

"That's what I heard. But it sounds kind of flaky to me. Do you know I adopted the poor thing?"

"How nice of you. Well, thanks for calling me, Tommi. That's all quite intriguing I'll have to say. Now I've gotta go." And she hung up. Most people would have loved to continue discussing such juicy gossip.

I felt quite satisfied. For one thing, how did Rhonda know that Joe purportedly tripped over the cat? It wasn't public knowledge. She could have found out from Joe's next-door neighbor, but somehow I doubted it.

Next I called Bernard.

"What's up?" he said when he answered.

"I think we can bring this to a head," I said. "What I need is some help from the police."

Before he could say a word I told him all the events that had unfolded since we'd been to his office. "I'm almost certain it was Rhonda or Steve or both who've tried to kill me. I spoke to Rhonda just now, and I'm certain one of them will try again. And probably tonight. Frank is staying here because he's worried about me. But, Bernard, he would be helpless against any kind of weapon. He hates guns and so do I. So we're defenseless. And I haven't told him that I planned to call you. Can you get the police to stake out my house?"

"I'll call the detective on the case right now and see

what I can do. In the meantime, arm yourself with a knife or scissors or something."

I got my large sewing shears out of the desk drawer which was in my bedroom and put them under my pillow. I decided to keep the light on as long as possible, sure that any intruder would wait until all the house was dark.

At ten o'clock Bernard called me back on my cell phone. "The cops have agreed to send a SWAT team. They'll run surveillance on both the front and back of your house. But you be damn careful."

"I'm armed with a nasty pair of scissors," I said. "Hope I don't have to use them."

There was no way I was going to sleep. About ten-thirty Frank came up the stairs. I heard water running in the bathroom and then the bedroom door close. His bedroom was on the back of the house and mine on the front. I didn't think Rhonda or Steve would know that Frank was staying with me. The parking in front of the condos was catch-as-catch-can and all spaces were available to anyone. It wasn't as if I had a strange car in my driveway. I assumed that whoever came would come in the front door. I'd put a bar in the sliding door so the only way to get in the back would be to break it, and that would make too much noise. The window over the sink in the kitchen had a storm window that would make it difficult if not impossible to get in that way. I'd been thinking about the day the gas jets were opened on my stove. I remembered back to the board meeting when Rhonda said there was a

NANCY GOTTER GATES   243

master key to the condos that the painters were using when they painted the doors. In her position as chairman of the board, it wouldn't be at all difficult to get hold of it. All she had to do was let herself in, or give it to Steve.

At eleven I finally got up the courage to turn off my light and open my bedroom door so I could hear any noises downstairs. I had 9-1-1 on speed dial and the phone was next to my bed, just in case the cops had changed their minds. My nerves were about to get the better of me.

I lay down on top of the bed covers fully clothed. Since I usually go to sleep pretty early every night, I had to fight to stay awake. Every once in a while I'd catch myself dozing off, and I'd force my eyes open. Finally I realized I couldn't remain in bed. I turned the secretarial chair I had at my desk so it faced out and sat in that, my eyes riveted on the dark space that was the bedroom door.

Time marched on. The illuminated clock on my nightstand was the only light in the room. I'd closed the mini-blinds at the window though I peeked out once or twice between the slats to check the street. Nothing. Absolutely nothing. It was going to be pretty embarrassing if I was wrong and no one showed up.

At two-forty-three I heard a faint noise from downstairs. I could tell it came from the front door which was at the bottom of the stairs. Someone was very stealthy, and I almost missed the sound. Thank God I hadn't used WD-40 on the squeaky hinge as I'd meant to do some time ago. Now I could hear soft footsteps on the uncarpeted stairs.

Shaking now, I pulled the scissors from under my pillow and held them in my fist, the sharp end pointing toward the door.

"Freeze!" I heard the clatter of many feet and voices yelling, "You're under arrest! Get down! Get down!"

I turned on the light beside my bed and ran to the top of the stairs, still holding the scissors. Cops in SWAT uniforms were handcuffing two people lying prone on my living room floor near the bottom of the stairs. Another had his gun trained on them. Frank came flying out of the back bedroom wearing a robe. His eyes were wild.

"What the hell?"

"It's the cops, Frank," I said, dropping the shears to my side so he wouldn't see them.

He looked at me accusingly. "Tommi?"

"Look, Frank, I knew they'd probably come after me again. I called Bernard and asked him to contact the police. I sure didn't want us to face them alone." I didn't tell him that I'd egged it on with a call to Rhonda.

Once the perps were successfully subdued, Frank and I went downstairs. Rhonda and Steve were being patted down, and one of the cops found a gun in Steve's pocket. They were read their rights and hustled out into the night to be taken to the police station.

Detective Arnold who had questioned me at the Kathleen Clay Edwards library branch following the death of Fulton Ridenhour remained behind. "Are you okay?" he asked us.

"Totally shook up," Frank answered. "I had no idea what was going down. Tommi, here, apparently set this up."

I grinned at him, hoping he wasn't too mad. But tough luck if he was.

Arnold looked at his watch. "It's late and you must be exhausted. Come into the station tomorrow and give a statement."

"Be glad to," I said.

"Sure," Frank said. "What time?"

"I'll let you get a little shuteye. How about ten?"

He left and Frank and I fell exhausted onto the sofa. The next thing I knew he had his arms around me in a bear hug. He pulled back, looked at me a minute, and then planted a long, passionate kiss on my mouth. Then he embraced me again. "You are so incorrigible," he said. "What am I ever going to do with you?"

I smiled. A smile filled with happiness, but also trepidation. "This is one package that is marked 'as is.' I've changed a lot since Bernard and I split. I don't let other people tell me what to do anymore. And I'm a lot happier for it. So take it or leave it, Frank."

He didn't hesitate. "I'll probably end up a basket case, but I'll take it, Tommi. I want you to be a part of my life."

"Okay," I said meekly.

He took my hand and led me back up the stairs.

TWENTY-TWO

WHEN THE COPS PUT ALL the pieces together, it turned out to be close to the way I had envisioned. Rhonda, Fulton, and Steve were working together on various scams. Rhonda was pretty much the brains, Steve the brawn, and Fulton knew legal angles. They had conspired on the suit over Sir Martingale, and Rhonda confirmed that they'd only meant for the dog to run away. Poor Bob and Shirley Hayes accidentally got caught up in it and almost had their lives ruined.

Rhonda agreed to tell all when the prosecutor offered her twenty-five to life instead of life without parole. She'd been the mastermind behind Fulton's death, but Steve was the muscle. She figured that the reenactment would pull all the spectators away from Fulton's tent, but the crowds would give the police hundreds of suspects. Steve had planned to kill him with a knife he had for sale in his tent, but on his way to Fulton's place, he stumbled upon Garland's sword lying on the ground. It had almost seemed preordained to him that he could cast suspicion on a reenactor.

When asked why she wanted to kill him, after all

he was making money for her, she said he'd blown his top when Joe Kernodle got the better of him. He blamed Rhonda for choosing him to be on our committee and told her he was going to get even by cutting her out of his scams. He and Steve would share all the profits. And she was afraid he was going to alert the cops to the fact she was cooking the books for the homeowners' association. When no one would volunteer to be the treasurer, she'd offered to handle them, assuring the board that since she didn't work, she had the time. And she was smart enough to know how to hide her embezzlement from a simple audit.

Since Steve had been involved with Fulton, she knew she had him under her thumb. He would do whatever she told him to do.

Like killing Joe Kernodle. When Rhonda found out that Joe had a PI looking into Fulton's background, she was scared he wouldn't stop there but would continue to dig and unearth the whole complicated mess. With Joe dead, she figured the PI would no longer be involved, thinking his was an accidental death.

She had access to that master key and let Steve into Joe's house while he was gone. Hiding in an upstairs bedroom, he waited till Joe came home and surprised him at the top of the stairs. He pushed him down the steps and made sure he was dead with a baseball bat in reserve in case he wasn't. He found Stacy, broke its poor little paw with the bat, and left her by Joe's body. Rhonda was adamant that everything look like an

accident since the police had set their sights on
Garland. She didn't want them to change their mind.

Unfortunately, Rhonda found out that I'd come into
the picture. She had called Constance shortly after
Garland was arrested and pretended concern, offering
to help in any way she could. Constance, in all innocence, told her that I was helping Bernard find out
other possible scenarios for the murder. I would never,
ever share that with Constance. She'd be devastated
if she knew she'd sicked Rhonda on me.

She also redid Fulton's ledger to show he only
shared his ill-gotten gains with Steve. She figured that
after I was dead, and she was determined to kill me,
the cops would go through his house again, find the
ledger, and arrest Steve. I'd always wondered why it
wasn't hidden more carefully. That would steer all
suspicion away from her.

As I suspected, Rhonda had placed the dead rat
behind the refrigerator which gave her the chance to
come in, whack me over the head, stab me, and steal
my purse and car, making it appear to be a robbery/at-
tempted murder. She really thought she'd killed me
when the wound bled so heavily. When that didn't
work, she got desperate and, using her master key
once more, entered my house and turned all the stove
burners on and blew out the flames. She couldn't have
been thinking clearly because, although it could have
blown up the house, the smell of the leaking gas had
alerted me. Because she was determined to make my
demise seem an accident, she made mistakes. She

may have been smart, but she could panic under pressure.

Steve, of course, couldn't deny his involvement after Rhonda finished telling all. There was one thing she didn't know about, and Bernard was curious as to why Steve had reported Fulton to the bar. It seemed so far-fetched for him to snitch on his partner in crime. But Steve admitted he did it to keep Fulton from getting uppity and dropping him from his circle. "If he became a lawyer, he'd just pal up with other crooked lawyers to run his scams and forget about me," he said. What a great world view he had!

Steve pleaded guilty to second-degree murder and also got twenty-five to life.

GARLAND, OF COURSE, was exonerated and the case against him dropped. The school welcomed him back, and the principal expressed regret that they'd had to keep him from teaching during his ordeal. "But you understand, I'm sure," he said. Garland agreed that he did. Fortunately he wasn't the kind to feel aggrieved and was thrilled to be back in the classroom.

As Frank and I had promised we recruited several others from the condo board and moved the Hayeses back to their home at the end of the month. Shirley spent the day at Chakras Day Spa while we unpacked and put everything away.

Stacy finally came out from under the bed in the guest room, and she and Tee were cautiously getting acquainted. They weren't best buddies yet, but they seemed to have made a truce.

I returned to work, and Frank began to search for a house. With the downturn in the housing market, he got a really good deal on a place on Honeysuckle Drive in Guilford Hills. It had three bedrooms, two baths, living room, kitchen, and a dining room upstairs, and a family room in the walk-out basement. Supported by brick pillars, a screened porch opened off the kitchen on the back and was surrounded by the upper branches of a host of Southern pines. He moved in the end of April and was able to enjoy the last of the dogwood blossoms and the azaleas that bloomed out in front. He'd always loved gardening so he chose a house over a condominium.

Since he was now living in town, Nina stayed with him while undergoing her treatments. This put her much closer to the hospital.

"This way he'll have supper on the table when he gets home from work," she said. "He's always spoiled me, so I'm going to spoil him a little bit. I hope you'll join us often for meals."

"Thanks, I will, now and then," I said.

I did want to see Nina occasionally, but I also was anxious to spend some private time with Frank. And he felt the same way. I finally got it all figured out.